DARK TIMES

A GLITCH IN TIME SAGA

BOOK TWO

LOIS FARLEY-RAY

PAGE PUBLISHING, INC.
Conneaut Lake, PA

First originally published by Page Publishing 2020

ISBN 978-1-64628-569-3 (pbk)
ISBN 978-1-64628-570-9 (digital)

Printed in the United States of America

This is dedicated to my husband, Roger Ray;
to my mom and dad, Shirley and Bill Farley.

PROLOGUE

The evil fog boiled like liquid in a witch's cauldron. Lost souls of poor choices surfaced in an attempt to break away, only to be sucked down once again. Their cries of sorrow were muffled in the darkness. The haze twisted, rolled, folded, and turned like clouds before a tornado.

"Asil Emit, don't get too comfortable. I am coming for you," the dark mist hissed.

CHAPTER 1

L isa Time (a.k.a. Asil Emit) lay on the beach and listened to the waves rush onto the sand and then slide back into the ocean. *Zoosh, zoosh, zoosh*, they sang. Presently, she lives on a tropical island called Time Central in the Pacific Ocean, but it wasn't that long ago that she lived in Michigan in a foster home.

Flies buzzed the seaweed that rolled up onto the shore, and gulls flew overhead. Lisa relaxed on a beach chair on the black, volcanic sand. She looked out at the Pacific Ocean as hermit crabs scurried about. One or two puffy clouds floated across the sky. Lisa filled her lungs with the fresh ocean air and released it with a sigh.

Life on the island offered many adventures, such as a daily swim in the ocean, surfing, mountain climbing, trail riding, or hang gliding. These activities helped to build the muscle that now hugged her once pencil-thin frame. Her frizzy, poodle hair had softened, and she had grown taller. Her feet no longer looked too big for her body. As a ten year old, she was a cutie.

It had been only eleven months since she witnessed the time glitch in Michigan that changed her life, and yet it seemed like a lifetime ago. Because of that one event, she could control time. Fast, slow, and even stop were easy to achieve; all that was needed was a command. Time travel, now that was trickier. That took concentration and focus on a destination and period of time. Then, like a crystal shatters sunlight to make rainbows, Lisa shatters images.

A smile touched her lips as she remembered her first trip. It was a complete accident. Lisa went to a prehistoric swamp with dinosaurs. A chuckle developed deep in her chest when she remembered her teacher had been a T. rex and the students had become velociraptors.

The whole time-control issue was really scary until Lisa met App. He was a new foreign-exchange student from Time Island. He seemed kind of odd with his fuzzy yellow hair, car-door ears, and big feet. But he knew about time travel and time control. He became her best friend. It was because of him she met her adopted parents, Time Glitch Master, better known as G-Master or G, and Miss Pinky. It was a very lucky day when she witnessed the time glitch.

Lisa closed her eyes, curled her toes into the sand, and listened. *Zoosh, zoosh, zoosh.* A warm, loving radiance surrounded her.

A disembodied voice said, "Hello, Asil, dear. How are you?"

She never opened her eyes. She almost purred, "Ahhhh. I remember you. You're the wise one who showed me the time glitch in Michigan."

"Yes, my dear, I am."

"Is something wrong?"

"Indeed there is. In seven weeks, six days, five hours, and four minutes, three time continuums will collide. Evil darkness from all three will combine like bubbles in dish soap and create a huge mass. Evil will be three times more powerful than at any other time. True freedom of choice will be lost."

"You are a very powerful being. Can't you control evil?"

"Alas, therein lies the problem. I know and understand time glitches, time bending, and wrinkles. They are constant and predictable. Humans are not predictable. They can be greedy, corrupt, angry, fearful, and hateful. These human traits create negative energy. Darkness consumes negativity like children collect Halloween candy. The more it has, the more it wants. The more it consumes, the faster it spreads."

A fly buzzed Lisa's face. She wiggled her nose and waved it away. "What can I do?"

"You can be at the point where the time glitches collide. Human weakness must be kept under control as much as possible."

"How do I do that?"

"Use what you have learned."

Lisa had learned a lot about time travel and repelling evil when she lived in Michigan. "What if I fail?"

"I have faith in you. I know that you will do your best. You won't disappoint me."

With that, the loving warmth receded, like the ocean waves after they rush to shore.

"But... Wait...!"

Lisa's eyes snapped open in time to see the warm light disappear overhead. Rainbow sprinkles softly floated down. They landed on her hair and face.

I need to talk to G-Master, said Lisa to herself. Towel in hand, she grabbed up her beach chair and ran as fast as the hot, loose sand would allow. She climbed the dune and disappeared into the jungle.

CHAPTER 2

The control room was so quiet, that a bee buzzing by the door sounded like a buzz saw. Lisa hit the door on the run. It slammed against the wall with a resounding boom.

"Where is G-Master?" barked Lisa. Her tone of voice was serious, as was the look on her face.

"I believe," replied the lead technician on duty in the time-control room, "that he and Pinky headed to lunch."

With a quick nod of her head, Lisa dropped her items, dashed out the door, and headed for the mess hall.

"Today's lunch is the very best," exclaimed G-Master to Pinky as they sat at the table by the window. "Chef sure knows how to make spaghetti and meat balls." G-Master smacked his lips and wound up another forkful of spaghetti noodles to scoop into his mouth.

"Give me a break," Pinky said as she dabbed the sides of her mouth with a pink napkin. "You know full well that you say that about every meal you eat. I think the only thing you don't like to eat is green olives."

"No one should like olives. For heaven sakes, they are salty, green, and have red-looking guck in the center. They look like eyeballs rolling around on the plate. Any sane person would feel the same way!"

Pinky just laughed at G-Master's reason. He always used the same one. Most everyone on the island could quote word for word his reason for not liking green olives.

Lisa sped into the room. She slowed long enough to spot G and then continued her mad dash to his table. The shiny floor made it difficult to stop. She slid past their table and had to back up.

She struggled to catch her breath. In between gasps of air, she said, "G-Master—huh—huh—huh—we need—huh, huh—to talk! Huh—something awful is going to happen! Huh—huh—huh."

"Can it wait until I have finished this scrumptious meal?" he said as he shoveled in another load.

He chuckled as the noodle spun around and around until he sucked the end into his mouth. He looked up at Lisa. All amusement melted from his face.

He dropped his fork back into his plate of spaghetti. "My dear, what is wrong?" His voice was filled with concern. "Come with me."

He took Lisa's arm and led her out the side door of the mess hall and down to his office. While Lisa caught her breath, he closed the office door.

G-Master took the chair across from her and said, "Tell me what has happened, girl, and don't leave anything out."

For the next quarter hour, Lisa explained all that she knew about the upcoming disaster, and he quietly listened. When she had finished, the room was full of silence. He removed his glasses that made his eyes look too big for his face. He wiped them on his shirt then rubbed the bridge of his nose while he thought. Setting the glasses back on his nose, he looked at the girl seated across from him.

With a heavy sigh G-Master asked, "Lisa, what do you think needs to be done?"

"Well, I need to be on location when the timeline continuums collide," said Lisa thoughtfully.

"That was my exact thought. However, you do know that this could be dangerous, right?"

"Yes."

"And you still want to do this?"

"Yes."

"Okay, let's make it so."

CHAPTER 3

In four weeks, three days, two hours, and one minute the three time continuums will collide.

The old cinder block building in Burton had been around for a long time. Four generations of families had passed through its halls. It looked more like a prison block than a school. The bars on the basement windows which kept kids from breaking out the glass added to the prison feel. The once-tall windows that allowed the maximum amount of light into the rooms were now cut in half, with the top section boarded off. It was a cost-cutting measure to keep the heating bill down. Lamb School was indeed old and tired.

Lisa and her best friend App opened the windowless double-steel doors and stepped inside. The doors banged shut behind them as they stepped into the hallway. The single row of fluorescent lights down the center of the hall had also fallen victim to cost-cutting measures. Every other light was on. Several of the lights blinked.

App and Lisa looked down the hall and then at each other. Should they go on or not?

App sniffed the air then made a face. "What is that smell?" he asked in a whispered voice.

Lisa sniffed, smiled, and said "That is floor wax, old books, paper, chalk dust, lunches left in lockers for a week or two, sweaty bodies, and old building. In short, that, my dear App, is the smell of education."

"Yuck," he replied.

They had just passed the first two classroom doors and had almost made it to the second set of fire doors when the bell rang. Classroom doors bust open and hordes of students filled the halls. Lisa and App backed up against the wall to watch. The teachers from rooms one and three stepped into the hall. According to the signs on the doors, they were Miss Mackie and Mr. Hub.

As they stood, supervising the hallway and talking, a student tried to run past. Without interrupting her conversation, Miss Mackie's arm reached out faster than a cobra could strike and latched on to the boy's neck. Like a dog coming to the end of a short chain, his head and shoulders stopped, but his feet kept going. Had Miss Mackie let go, he would have landed flat on his back.

Once he had regained his feet, Miss Mackie gave him a bit of a shake and turned him loose. He stood for a second and then said, "Yes, ma'am, next time I will walk!"

Her only acknowledgment of the boy's statement was a slight nod of her head as she finished her conversation with Mr. Hub. She turned and looked at App and Lisa standing in the hall. "Don't be late for class," she said in a scratchy voice.

It wasn't until she turned toward them that they saw the burn scar that marked the side of her old, wrinkly face. Her sharp eyes missed nothing when she looked at them. Then she walked into her room and grabbed the doorknob. As she closed the door, they could hear her screech at the second-period students, "*Shut up* and *sit down!*"

"Whoa! That is one scary lady," whispered Lisa as she gave a shiver. "I hope I never have a run in with her."

"Yeah, she does seem that way on the surface," replied App. "The strange thing is, she has a very kind aura. She really believes that she is helping. But you're right. I wouldn't want to get her angry at me."

The halls had cleared, and the bell rang. They started through the fire door toward the office when they heard "*Halt!*" Lisa and App stopped, looked at each other, and turned to see a nerdy-looking boy standing behind them. His dusty brown hair was buzzcut. He wore a striped shirt with a pocket protector filled with pens. His polyester pants were a bit too short, showing white tube socks. He held a clip-board, with tickets clamped on it.

"Sorry, guys, I am going to have to give you a ticket," said the boy.

"Great, a ticket for what? A movie, concert, or something free?" asked App, holding out his hand.

Lisa touched App's arm. "I don't think it is that kind of ticket. I think it is a bad thing."

"Bad? How can it be a bad ticket? We just got here!"

"According to the school code of conduct, you are delinquent in reporting to class. Therefore, I must issue a ticket for detention," he said with authority.

Then with a kind of smile on his face, he said, "I know this is too bad for you, but this is the first time I have been able to write a ticket since I have had this job."

"How long have you had this job?" asked Lisa.

"This is my second year."

"I hate to break the news to you, buddy, but we are not enrolled in this school yet," App informed him.

"Oh, rats. That's a disappointment. Well, let me welcome you to Lamb School. My name is Arthur," he said as he shook their hands.

"Nice to meet you, Arthur. My name is App, and this is my sister, Lisa," he lied.

The sound of running feet could be heard near the intersection of the north-south hall and the east-west hall.

"Quick, you can give that guy a ticket," said App.

"No, I can't give him a ticket. He is an athlete."

"What difference does that make? He's delinquent for class too."

"Yes, I know," he sighed. "But athletes run too fast for me to catch."

Under her breath, Lisa said, "Time slow in the north hall only." Aloud, she said, "Look, he is running slowly. Hurry, I think you can catch him."

"Holy cow," Arthur exclaimed and took off down the hall.

Once he caught up with the student, Lisa said in a quiet voice, "Normal time in the north hall."

"I think you might have made his day," App said thoughtfully.

They continued their journey to the office to enroll in the school.

14

CHAPTER 4

L ater that day, Lisa and App entered the cafeteria. With trays in their hands, they surveyed the seating arrangements.

"Why are all the students sitting in different groups?" inquired App.

"That group over there," Lisa said, pointing toward the windows, "is the popular students, the athletic type, and cheerleaders. Everyone wants to be friends with them." She nodded in the direction of another band of kids. "Those are the tough guys. Everyone stays away from them except for the ones that want to be tough guys too. The 'wannabe tough guys' are the students that are always trying to be accepted by them. They are usually in trouble. Some kids will do anything to be accepted."

"What about that cluster of students over there?" asked App as he pointed to the far corner.

"Those are the smart kids. They're doing their homework right now."

"What about the ones sitting alone?"

"I know all about that group of students. I was one of them. They are the misfits. Maybe they look different. Maybe they don't have the right kind of clothes. They might be nerdy, too fat or thin, smell bad, or maybe there is no reason that they are excluded from the group. They simply don't fit in."

"I don't understand this! We're not like this at home."

"I know."

"So how do we start to make friends?"

"Good question. The nerds and misfits are the easiest group to join. They want to have friends and are willing to accept others. But once we are accepted by them, we won't be able to blend in with the popular kids. If we start with the most popular group, then the others won't trust us."

"So what should we do?"

"I think we should—"

The double doors behind App and Lisa slammed open and almost knocked App off his feet. The commotion caught everyone's attention as Arthur hustled into the cafeteria with his clipboard and delinquent tickets.

"Hey, guys," he called to Lisa and App. "You were right. I was able to catch up with that athletic jock, and I gave him a ticket. Man, was he mad."

As if on cue, an evil mist appeared between the cracks in the ceiling tile. It was devilish black, and it whirled about the room one time. It found its victim in Bull and wrapped around his neck. Only Lisa and App witnessed its presence. They shivered in response.

The mist took effect. His face was set and hard with his teeth clinched. Bull roared up out of this seat and started toward them. "You two! Are you the reason I ended up with a detention? When I get my hands on you, I am going to rip you to pieces," Bull growled as he thundered across the room.

The evil mist helped fuel Bull's agitation. The more he became aggressive and riled, the darker the swirling mist became. It increased Bull's rage with a hiss of encouragement.

While on the football field, everyone cheered Bull for his aggressiveness. He was a hero for the winning team. In the lunch room, it was a completely different story. Chairs flipped over, lunch trays crashed to the floor, and girls squealed as they hurried to get away from him.

App elbowed Lisa into action.

"Time stop," she whispered. "Umm, I guess that answered that question. We will make friends with the outcasts first," said Lisa. "But before we even think of that, we have to get out of here before someone gets hurt, and by someone, I mean us. You grab one of Arthur's arms, and I'll grab the other. Let's get out of here."

They dragged Arthur to the home-school councilor's office and stood him in the corner.

Lisa commanded, "Normal time."

In a daze, Arthur slid to the floor in a lump. He finally sat up and shook his head a time or two. He looked around the office and then at Lisa and App. "Where am I? How did I get here? What is going on? I thought I was in the lunch room."

"Yes, you were in the lunchroom. You must have blacked out when you saw Bull coming at us. You need to stay here until the home-school councilor checks you out. Okay?" said App.

"Yeah, I think that might be a good idea," said Arthur, placing a hand to the side of his head, "I really don't think I feel so good. I sure don't know how I got here!"

App and Lisa left him in the office and hurried back to the lunchroom.

CHAPTER 5

Meanwhile, back in the lunchroom, Bull pulled up short. He spun to the left, and then again to the right. "Where are they?" he bellowed to the crowd of students around him.

He lifted a chair over his head and slammed it against the wall. The wooden seat splintered into toothpicks on impact. Snarling like a grizzly bear, he turned, looking for something else to throw. More chairs and a table were added to the splinter pile.

Students rushed to escape. Teachers tried to supervise the students as they left the room. Doors and windows were quick exits outside. With their frantic attempt to get away, students were knocked to the floor or pushed out of the way. Sirens wailed as police cars and fire trucks neared the building.

"Where are they? Those little rats. *No one.* Do you hear me? *No one* gives me a detention," raged Bull. Spittle spayed from his mouth as he spun in circles, looking for them. "That little nerd and his two geeky friends are going to pay for this. Where are they hiding? Come on out, you ugly little rats." He picked up a chair and slammed it against the wall.

Bull was still in full rage when the first policeman arrived on the scene. He carefully approached Bull. In a soothing, calming voice, the officer said, "Son, let's put the chair down and talk about this. I can see you are very upset. If you tell me what the problem is, maybe we can work this out."

Bull hesitated a moment. He lowered the chair he held but not all the way. His eyes lost some of the dazed look they held a moment ago.

The dreadful mist circled, swirled, and churned tighter and firmer around Bull. It softly hissed, "Don't listen to his trash talk. The only way to get what you want is to take it. Take it! Come on, take it. You can do it."

A gray, glassy glaze returned to his eyes. He lifted the chair higher, and with the strength of what seemed like an elephant, he heaved it toward the officer. The chair hit the wall and exploded on impact. Wood shrapnel flew in all directions.

A second officer came up behind him and grabbed him. Bull flipped him over his shoulder. A third officer zapped him with a taser gun. Bull went down like a fallen tree. It took four officers to get him cuffed and strapped on the gurney. Then he was rushed away to the hospital.

CHAPTER 6

Mr. Zornet was a thin, wispy, little man. He had a long pointy nose and red complexion. He always walked around with his hands clasped together near his chest, with his shoulders slumped forward. He looked more like an undertaker greeting visitors at the door of a funeral home than a teacher.

He happened to be in the hall when he saw Arthur hustle into the lunchroom. He heard him talk to Lisa and App. Mr. Zornet stopped outside the door. The clamor of lunchroom sounded normal until he heard the first chair shatter against the wall.

Mr. Zornet listened and waited. The next thing he knew, Lisa and App came toward him from the office. He looked at the lunchroom door and then at the two students. "You two, stop right there."

Lisa and App didn't even notice Zornet standing in the hall. They jolted to a stop in front of him.

"What is going on here? I just saw you in the lunchroom with Arthur. What are you doing coming from the office?"

Lisa and App were speechless.

Mr. Zornet eyed them closely. "I caught you, didn't I?"

Rubbing his hands together as he circled them like a cat with a mouse. Squinting his eyes, he studied them, as though they were amoeba under a microscope. "Yes, I do believe I have caught you red-handed. The question remains, what were you doing in two places at once? I shall enjoy figuring this one out."

A policeman and firefighter interrupted Mr. Zornet's interrogation. "Everyone out! We are clearing the building. You, students, you need to follow this firefighter to a safer location," came the order from the officer in charge.

Mr. Zornet whispered to Lisa and App as they quickly moved away, "We shall finish this conversation at a later date." To the policeman, he said, "Can I be of assistance?"

It was as if Mr. Zornet had never said a word. The officer kept right on, walking as though he was the only one in the hall.

"Humph," mumbled Mr. Z, and he walked away.

CHAPTER 7

B efore G-Master left Time Island, he gave Mathman an assignment that might help them pinpoint the evil's attack.

"We know that the three timelines are going to collide. We know that it will happen in seven weeks, six days, four hours, and forty minutes. We also know that one of the times will be ours. We can do research to find out when it happened the first time. What we don't know is when it will happen again. Is there any way you can calculate that for us?" asked G-Master.

"Well now, let me see if I…" Mathman instantly scribbled numbers in a new notebook and started running mathematical calculations.

G-Master did not try to interrupt him. Once on a project, he sometimes didn't talk to anyone for hours or days.

That happened over four weeks ago, and G-Master still hadn't heard anything from Mathman.

"Dagnabbit, what is he doing? He should have an answer by now. If we could check the other two time continuums, we would better know where we should concentrate our efforts." G-Master fussed to himself as he took his glasses off to rub the bridge of his nose.

"Just stay calm, dear. Getting all worked up is not going to help," advised Pinky as she monitored the news channels for current events. "If anyone can figure out the other time periods, it will be Mathman."

CHAPTER 8

"We almost got caught yesterday," App said as he and Lisa walked to school.

"I know. We need to be more careful. Everything happened so fast, I forgot to check," replied Lisa.

"It wasn't just your fault. I wanted to get out of there as fast as possible too."

"Okay, today's plan is try to blend in. Stay out of the way. How does that sound?"

"Works for me."

The bell rang and the students entered the building. Lisa and App were swept up in the crowd of students. Miss Mackie and Mr. Hub stood at their posts as the students entered. Miss Mackie never even turned and looked, but as Lisa walked by, her wrinkled, bony hand snatched Lisa's arm. She held on to her until almost everyone was out of the hall. App tried to stay back and wait for Lisa, but Miss Mackie gave him "the teacher stare." He moved on with the crowd.

Miss Mackie backed Lisa up to the wall and said, loud enough that only Lisa could hear, "You're the one, aren't you?"

"Pardon?"

"You're the one, aren't you?"

"Well, I am a new student. I started yesterday."

"That's not what I mean and you know it."

"I don't mean to be disrespectful, ma'am, but I don't know what you are talking about."

"So that's the way it is going to be, is it?" said Miss Mackie as she released Lisa's arm. "Okay, you better get to class."

Lisa hurried through the fire doors and found App waiting for her.

"What was that all about?"

"I don't know. It is almost like she knows something but won't say what. This is very strange."

They hurried to their classrooms.

CHAPTER 9

Mr. Zornet stood at the top of the steps of the second floor in his undertaker stance. The arched window over the stairs was the only tall window that wasn't boarded up. It was the perfect place to keep watch.

Hands folded together close to his chest, he surveyed the sidewalk. Finally, he saw them approach the building. They stood a little away from the other students, and when the bell rang, they blended into the crowd and disappeared into the door.

Mr. Zornet scurried from the window to the balcony that looked down over the stairs. He recognized App's fuzzy yellow hair and big ears as soon as they came into view. Right behind App, Lisa's soft light-brown curly locks came into view. When Miss Mackie grabbed Lisa by the arm and placed her against the wall, Mr. Zornet's eyes grew large. A smile-smirk touched his lips, and he wrung his hands together much as child might on Christmas morning.

"Wow! I knew it. I knew Mackie was an odd duck. She must be connected to those two somehow. I never did believe those stories that her face was burned in a fire while trying to save students," he said to himself. "I bet she is a witch."

"Are you talking to me, sir?" said Stinky timidly.

"What makes you think I was talking to you?"

"Well, sir," Stinky said, looking around, "you and I are the only ones left on the steps. I didn't think you were talking to yourself. Or are you?"

"Oh, shut up and get to class," grouched Zornet as he shuffled off to his own classroom.

CHAPTER 10

The staff at Lamb School was edgy after Wednesday's problem in the lunchroom. But the morning progressed without any problems. App and Lisa noticed that Mr. Zornet was always nearby.

At lunchtime, Lisa and App met up at the lunch counter. They made their selections and headed to the eating area.

"Where should we sit?" asked App.

Arthur was seated with his group of misfit friends. When he saw them enter, he jumped up and yelled across the room.

"Hey, guys, come and join us."

When Lisa and App didn't react, he waved and yelled louder, "App, Lisa, come and join us. I saved you a seat."

"Question answered," stated Lisa.

They cut across the cafeteria between the rows of tables. The smart kids never looked up from their work. Bull's teammates growled at them as they passed their table. The cheerleaders and popular students made a point of looking them up and down, then they looked away. The thugs followed them with their eyes when they passed.

"Hey, look. It's the kid with the yellow rug for hair," snickered one of the thugs.

"His ears are so big, I wonder if he can fly like Dumbo the Elephant?" the girl with the purple hair said as she blew a bubble.

"Ahh, I think that is Jumbo the Elephant," said the guy sitting next to her.

"No, this one is Dumbo." She laughed.

"And look, it's the good witch, Glenda, leading him around. Isn't that just so sweet? Are you afraid he will get lost on his own?" said the girl with the long, black hair dressed in emo clothes.

Lisa whispered to App once they had passed that table, "See, I told you this would happen."

CHAPTER 11

Lisa and App walked up to the table where Arthur and his friends sat. Arthur pointed to the two empty chairs and made a motion for them to sit down.

"Hey, guys, I want you to meet App and Lisa. They saved my life when Bull went whacko the other day," said Arthur to his small band of friends.

"Nice to meet you. My name is Blossom," said the girl sitting next to Arthur. "I heard what that emo girl said about you as you walked by that table. Her name is Spooky. Just ignore her. She is a mean one. Everyone knows it. She runs with a mean crowd. One time she teased me about being fat and having acne. I was so upset, I started to cry. She really thought that was funny. I don't know what would have happened if Pepper hadn't stepped up and stopped her…"

Whop—an orange peel hit Blossom upside the head. She wiped the side of her face and looked at Carlos. "What did you do that for?"

"Shut up, man," exploded Carlos. "We don't know these people. They don't need to know everything about us."

"Come on, Carlos, give it a rest. Not everyone is out to get you because you are the only Hispanic in school. Give these newbies a chance. They saved Arthur's life. That's good enough for me," said Stinky.

Stinky turned and looked at Lisa and App. "Just so you know, Stinky is my nick name. My real name is Walt, but my mom puts garlic and other spices in almost everything we eat. Consequently I smell like garlic most of the time. Feel free to call me Stinky. Everyone does. It's nice meeting you," he said as he gave them both a fist bump.

"If you will excuse me," interrupted Blossom. "Carlos, don't you ever throw anything at me again. I will get even with you."

Carlos shrugged and smirked.

"I was not finished telling Lisa and App about how Pepper helped me." Blossom turned back to the others. "Pepper use to be a cheerleader and one of the most popular girls in school. But once she stood up for me, she was shunned. I am sorry that she lost her status with the others, but I am grateful for her friendship every day."

Pepper had a flawless mocha complexion. Her face was framed with shoulder-length hair, and her clothes were perfect.

"I only did what needed to be done," she said, looking a bit embarrassed by all of Blossom's praise.

CHAPTER 12

N ow that we have the introductions out of the way, I have a juicy rumor to share," announced Stinky. He had everyone's full attention.

"This morning, as I was walking up the steps, I saw Mr. Zornet hanging over the staircase railing, watching someone and talking to himself. When I asked if he was talking to me, he acted all befuddled-like and told me to go to class."

"Man, stop stalling, just tell us what he said," grumbled Carlos as he broke up his foam lunch tray.

"Well, first he said that Miss Mackie was—umm—how did he put it? Oh yeah, he said she was an odd duck. Next he said she was connected to 'those two' somehow. I couldn't see over the railing to see who he was talking about. Then he mumbled something about her face scars and that maybe she was a witch."

"Lisa, are you cold? I just saw you shiver," observed Pepper.

"Me? No. The thought of being connected to Miss Mackie in any way gives me the shivers."

"That's the truth," agreed Blossom. "Walking by her room gives me the creeps."

"Everyone here is in agreement with that," added Arthur.

"I thought he had something new to tell us. Everyone knows that about Mackie," proclaimed Carlos, rolling his eyes.

"Yeah, but who are the two she is connected with? That is the question. Who would want to be connected with her? She is scary," stated Stinky.

CHAPTER 13

Spooky wore black clothes. She dyed her chestnut hair a flat black. Eight piercings adorned her ears, eyebrows, and nose. Black eye makeup, lipstick, and nail polish completed her goth look although sometimes she did use shocking-purple or bloodred nail polish to spice things up.

Spooky was not emotionally impaired as the label emo implied. It was better to be an emo though than to become an invisible nothing. Spooky also knew that a lot of her classmates were afraid of her. That was good. It gave her a power over them. Did it mean that she would have to get into a few scraps? Yes, that was okay. Did it mean making that fat Blossom girl cry? Yes, but so what? Spooky had shed rivers of tears too. She had worked hard building her image and was proud of it.

While eating lunch, Spooky observed that the newbies had been accepted by the misfits.

Isn't that just peachy, she thought. *It might just be time to become acquainted with these new students.*

After about twenty minutes, the new girl got up from the table and headed toward the restroom.

Hmmm, this might be the perfect time, she thought with a wicked grin.

Spooky waited a few minutes and then followed her into the restroom.

CHAPTER 14

L isa did a quick check to be sure she was alone before hustling into the last stall and locking the door. There wasn't much time.

Just like a crystal can capture sunlight and fracture it into individual colors, Lisa's mind could do the same thing to time and space. By concentrating, she could create an opening in the continuum, causing what she was looking at appear to be splintered. Stepping through this shattered image, she could go wherever she wanted.

She ended up in the kitchen of the home where she and App were staying with Pinky and G-Master. She tapped Pinky on the shoulder.

"Pinky."

"Ahhhhh!" screamed Pinky. "Girl, you scare the snot out of me every time you materialize out of nowhere."

"Sorry, but I don't have much time. Would you do a background check on Miss Ismay Mackie and Mr. Lester Zornet, please? I have to get back."

With that, Lisa disappeared from the kitchen and back to the restroom stall at school.

Upon her arrival she heard, "Where are you? Come out, come out, wherever you are," followed by pounding on the door.

"Excuse me, but I am in this stall."

"Duh, don't you think I know that? Why else would I be pounding on this door?"

"The other stalls are empty if you are in a hurry."

"Listen, sweet cheeks, me and you need to have us a little chit-chat. You can come out, or I can rip the door off and come…"

Lisa opened the door and stepped out before Spooky had a chance to finish what she was saying. They stood nose to nose.

"Do you have a problem?" asked Lisa.

"Ahhhhh," stammered Spooky.

"That's what I thought. Now excuse me. I have somewhere I need to be." Lisa breezed out the bathroom door and over to the table of misfits without looking back.

CHAPTER 15

S pooky's main defense was to intimidate and scare others. So when the stall door opened and Lisa stepped into her personal space, made direct eye contact, and didn't back away, Spooky was startled. She stood and watched Lisa as she left the restroom.

"What the heck just happened?"

No one had ever turned their back to her and just walked away. She eased the door open to watch Lisa return to the misfit table.

The bell rang. Students, including Spooky, headed back to class.

CHAPTER 16

Gym was Lisa's last class. She was very good at sports, and she was in great shape. What wasn't so fun was having to change clothes and take showers as a group. It reminded her too much of her life in foster care and orphanages.

Lisa changed quickly and scooted out of the locker room. Once in the gym, she waited in line, like everyone else, for class to start. Miss Mackie hustled into the gym.

"Okay, class, I am subbing for Miss Wize. She had an emergency and had to leave early. So shut up and listen. I don't care how she runs this class. I don't care what her rules are. I don't care what her plans are. We are going to play kickball."

The students numbered off into two teams. The ones were up to kick first and the twos went to outfield. The first kicker kicked a home run. The second kicker only made it to first base.

The game was soon four-to-four, and the bases were loaded. Everyone was into the game. The teams screamed and trash-talked at each other. Miss Mackie tooted on her whistle to keep control.

Blossom was next in line, and Lisa was behind her. Blossom was almost in tears. "I don't want to do this. I'm not any good at sports. I can't kick and I can't run."

"Just do your best," encouraged Lisa.

Tweeeeet. Ismay blew the whistle. "Kicker, get up there and let's play ball. We don't have all day," yelled Miss Mackie as she walked toward first base.

The pitcher rolled the ball, and Blossom kicked as hard as she could. The airborne ball made a direct line toward Miss Mackie and slapped her upside the head. The textured surface of the rubber ball stuck to Miss Mackie's gray wig. As the ball ricocheted off her head, it took the wig with it. The ball hit the floor and rolled, dragging the wig with it.

Mr. Teeterman, the principal, always checked on classes that had subs. He stepped into the gym to see how well the class was behaving. He saw a small gray-haired dog chasing the ball across the floor. "Get that dog out of here at once. Who does that dog belong to? Here, puppy, p—" he shouted as he ran after it.

Miss Mackie also chased the wigged ball. Her naked head had a few stray strands of hair flapping in the breeze as she ran.

"Time stop!"

Lisa went after the wigged ball. She snatched it up and separated the wig from the ball. She placed the ball near Mr. Teeterman's hands, and the wig, she took to Miss Mackie. Lisa combed her fingers through the hair to remove some of the tangles and floor dust. She took care in adjusting the wig so it would fit just right. She noticed the teacher's eyes following her movement.

Lisa whispered, "How could this be? How can you move your eyes? When time stands still, everyone freezes unless you are from Time Island."

Shaking her head, Lisa hurried back to where she should be.

"Normal time."

"—uppy," continued Mr. Teeterman.

The principal, catching a ball, yelling "Here, puppy! Here puppy!" was beyond hilarious. The kids howled with laughter. There was so much noise that the security guard arrived to be sure everything was okay.

Miss Mackie turned and made direct eye contact with Lisa. She said not word but blinked her eyes and gave a slight nod of her head. Miss Mackie looked away and blew her whistle. *Tweeeeet, tweeeet, tweeeeeeeeet.*

CHAPTER 17

On Friday evening, the kitchen was filled with the good smells of Pinky's cooking. Chicken sizzled in a large cast-iron frying pan. Homemade cornbread had just come out of the oven, and green beans boiled on the stove. Everyone hovered nearby. They didn't have to be called twice to the table.

"Dinner is served," called Pinky as she placed the food on the table.

G-Master, sitting at the head of the table, helped himself to a drumstick before passing the plate to his left.

"We have a lot to discuss," he said as he bit into a chicken leg. "Yum, yum. This is the best meal ever."

Pinky just smiled because G-Master said that same thing at every meal. After a few minutes of knives and forks clinking on glass plates, Pinky asked, "Okay, so what do we know so far?"

App wiped his hands on a napkin. "Miss Mackie stopped Lisa and asked if she was the one, whatever the heck that meant. Then at lunch, Stinky—"

"Stinky? Who names their kid Stinky?" asked G as he stuffed a large buttery piece of cornbread into his mouth. Butter dribbled off his chin and fingers.

With a heavy sigh, Pinky said, "Now, dear, we don't need to know why he's called Stinky."

"Well, I suppose that is true, but come on…Stinky?"

"App, please continue with your story."

"As I was saying, Stinky heard Mr. Zornet talking to himself, saying that Mackie was a witch and that she must be connected to them somehow."

G and Pinky looked at App.

"Connected to whom?" asked Pinky.

"That's just it. We don't know for sure, but we think he was talking about App and me," answered Lisa. "That is the reason for my pop-in visit today. Who are Lester Zornet and Ismay Mackie? Is there a connection? Plus, a very strange thing happened today, when Blossom knocked Miss Mackie's wig off during gym class."

"Knocked her wig off! That is just too funny," hooted App. "I would have loved to have seen that!"

"Yes, now it does seem kind of funny. But at the time, I felt sorry for her. It was a very embarrassing situation for her and the principal."

App looked a bit confused. "Why should Teeterman be embarrassed by Mackie's wig?"

"Mr. Teeterman walked in just after it happened and thought the wig was a dog chasing the ball. So he chased after the dog. I had to do something."

"*What?*" App shouted. He laughed so hard, he pounded on the table. "He thought it was a dog chasing the ball? Stop, I can't breathe." App rocked back and forth in his chair as he tried to catch his breath. "I can't believe it. Nothing that good ever happens in my classes."

Pinky brought them back to topic. "Okay, you two, let's stay focused."

"Oh yes," said Lisa. "Sorry. Anyway, I froze time to get the wig back and on her head before Teeterman could get his hands on it. She was frozen like everyone else, but she watched me. Is she from Time Island?"

The room went silent. Three pairs of serious eyes stared at her. She fidgeted under their intense gazes.

"Are you sure?" said G.

"Yes, sir. When I returned time to normal, she gave me a slow blink and a slight nod of her head. How was she able to do that? What does that mean?"

"It means," stated G-Master, "there must be some truth to the rumors."

"I did the background check you asked for," said Pinky. "I couldn't find any connection between Zornet and Mackie. In fact, I couldn't find anything on Ismay Mackie."

CHAPTER 18

*R*ing, *Ring, Ring.* The phone interrupted their conversation.
Pinky got up and answered the phone. "Time household. What? Oh yes, he is here." Pinky looked excited. "It's Mathman. He has some projections for you."

"Put him on speaker," said G-Master.

"Hi G. I have come up with the two projected dates that you requested. All I had to do was—"

"Whoa! I don't care how you got the answer. I wouldn't understand anyway." G took his glasses off and rubbed the bridge of his nose. "Just tell us what they are. Wait a second, I need to get a pencil and paper." G hustled to the desk and grabbed what he needed. "Okay, ready when you are."

"It looks like the dates are October 30, 1870; October 30, 2020; and October 30, 2170. I could be off a day or two one way or the other, but…"

"A day or two, one way or the other, won't make that much difference, I don't think. We can already see traces of unusual happenings here, and we are still a few weeks away. This is great information, Mathman. Thank you for your help," said Lisa.

CHAPTER 19

In the early hours on Saturday morning, Pinky hurried out of the bedroom and headed to the kitchen. She hummed a song as she walked. She came to a skidding stop when she saw all the stuff piled on the table. "How can I fix breakfast for you with all this mess in my kitchen?"

"Not a problem, dear. We have already eaten. I wanted to let you sleep a little longer. I know you were up most of the night, fussing about this trip," said G-Master. He walked over and put his arm around her shoulder.

Lisa and App hardly noticed Pinky's arrival in the kitchen. They were sorting through the survival items that were spread out on the table. It was difficult deciding what they would need to take with them on their journey.

"We should take a modern map of the area and a map overlay of the same area of Michigan in 1869. It will give us an idea of where we are," said Lisa.

"I concur with that. We will also need flashlights, binoculars, an army knife, and pepper spray for protection," added App.

"What about food, camping equipment, and other such items?" asked Pinky from the doorway. "It is late October. It can get mighty cold at night, and you don't know where you will stay."

"Wait a minute. Don't forget that those items have not been invented yet during that time period. You will stick out like a sore thumb if you show up with all that modern equipment," observed G.

Lisa scratched her head and said, "I have been thinking the same thing. However, we have to be prepared for any situation."

Pinky looked like a mother bear when she closed in on G. She placed her left hand on her hip and shook her right index finger in his face.

"Now you listen to me, G. You are not sending these two babies off without supplies," stated Pinky.

"It's okay," interrupted Lisa as she stepped between them before they could get into a long argument. "Look, we can take all that we can safely carry. When we get there, we can find a safe place to hide our extra supplies then take only what we think we will need for the moment."

Pinky and G stopped arguing and looked at Lisa.

"Perfect," they said at the same time.

Once everything was secured in their packs, they made their way to the garage to load up the car. G-Master backed the car out of the garage and pointed it in the direction of the school. Pinky sat in the front seat next to him, dabbing a stray tear from her eyes. Lisa and App squeezed into the back seat with the packs.

Taking a deep breath and sighing, Pinky said, "You don't have to do this, you know. Please, let's reconsider this outing."

G reached over and took Pinky's hand and gave it a gentle squeeze.

Keeping his eyes on the road, he said, "We know that the school is ground zero for the timeline overlap, so it is a good place to start your journey."

The streets were quiet under a clear sky. G parked the car about half a block away from Lamb School. The frost-covered grass crunched beneath their feet. A full moon cast their four shadows as they made their way to the school's front door, whereupon G took two packages out of the pockets of his coat.

"This may be an unnecessary precaution, but I will feel better if you had these items." He handed Lisa a bottle of holy water and a bag of salt to App. "These items will help protect you when you face evil. Evil can't cross over the salt. You can draw a circle on the ground with the salt and stand in the circle to keep evil away. The holy water can be sprinkled to drive the evil away.

Pinky fussed at Lisa, "Take care of yourself, sweetheart. Don't take any unnecessary risks. You hear me?"

"We won't," replied Lisa.

Then Lisa gave Pinky a hug and turned to G-master.

"I will do my best, sir. I don't want to disappoint you."

"Child, you can't disappoint me," G said. "I am very proud of you."

App gave Pinky a bear hug. "I'll keep a close eye on Lisa. You take care of G while we're gone. He tries to act tough, but deep down, I know he is a marshmallow."

Pinky smiled and said, "You are so right, but don't tell anyone. Be careful. You understand?"

"Yes, ma'am." App smiled. He stepped up and shook G's hand. They didn't say anything. They nodded to each other and App stepped away.

Lisa took App's hand, and with her mind, she bent time. The plane of space in front of them splintered into thousands of reflective crystals. Lisa stepped through first and App followed. The portal disappeared as soon as they did.

"They will be okay, won't they?"

"I hope so," commented G in a quiet voice. He took Pinky's hand, and they turned and walked to the car.

Pinky sniffled quietly.

Chapter 20

October 29, 1870

"John Henry, are you about ready to leave?" called Hattie from the porch of the small home.

John Henry stood six-foot-four, and when he stood by his wife, he looked like a giant. His arms and legs were as big and strong as oak trees. He was as gentle as a kitten with the ones he loved. He walked over to the porch, scooped her up in his arms, and twirled in a circle.

Hattie giggled like a child and swatted him on the shoulder. "Put me down, you silly ox." She laughed. "You need to get to the train depot to drop off the iron orders. I have a list of items I need from Murphy's Mercantile. Will you have time to pick them up?"

His skin was as black as the coal he used in his blacksmith shop. His teeth were white against his skin as he smiled at her and said, "For you, my sweet pea, I will make time." He placed her back on the porch and took the list from her hand.

"Wait a minute." She ran back into the house and came back out with a basket. "I packed a lunch for you. I can't have you falling over for the lack of food before you get back."

John Henry beamed at her as he took the basket from her hand. He walked over to the buckboard and placed it in the back.

He placed his foot on the axle behind the front wheel and swung up onto the wagon.

"Get up, Ole Mule," he said, tapping the driving lines on the mule's rump. One wave to Hattie and he was off down the trail to town. Rusty, his red-bone coonhound, followed along.

CHAPTER 21

The sun was bright, but the air was crisp and cool. Ole Mule never moved faster than a slow mosey. As a result, it took them an hour and a half to get to the depot.

The trees along the trail were a blaze of colors. The red leaves were so brilliant, they looked to be on fire, and the yellows dazzled in the sunshine. The fields had been harvested, and the ground tilled under. John Henry took in a large breath of fresh air and sighed.

The train depot was his first stop. He called out to the station manager, "Where shall I drop the wagon for unloading and loading?"

"Take it down to the water tower. You can water the mule there and tie him to the hitching post."

"Thanks."

He parked the wagon near the tracks and unhitched Ole Mule. He took the bridle off and hung it on one of Ole Mule's hames. He watered him and tied him to a hitching post for a nice rest.

Two blocks away was Murphy's Mercantile. He walked up the steps and opened the door. It was full of people.

"Did you hear that the school burned to the ground?"

"My Ben told me the teacher was able to get all the children out safely."

"One student didn't make it."

"What?"

"Who didn't make it?"

"Ted Wilber's kid, Webster."

"Oh my goodness, his poor mother."

"He was the wild kid, wasn't he? Every time he came into the store, he stole candy or a pickle out of the barrel. I heard the teacher got burned pretty bad."

"I heard that too. The burn was on the side of her face."

"This is just a real mess. Now we will have to build a new school. I bet it was carelessness."

"The real question is, what started the fire?"

"My Eli said he heard someone say that it wasn't the pot-belly stove. It was the only thing that wasn't burned."

"Well, my friend heard from her friend that Miss Mackie, the school teacher, said that a black mist came in from the woods across the street. So it must be true," came a report from the lady wearing a purple hat with a large feather in it.

John Henry observed this exchange. He shook his head then interrupted, "Sorry to disturb you, but can I get an order filled?"

The clerk looked up with surprise. "Oh, I didn't hear you come in, John Henry. Of course I can fill your order. When will you need it?"

"I'd like to leave after the 1:45 train. Would that be possible?"

"No problem."

"Thanks."

He turned to go.

"Wait! Wait a minute," called the hat lady. She marched right up to John Henry. She had to tilt her head back so she could look up at his face. "You came through those woods today. Did you see an evil black mist?" Eyes wide, she waited for and answer.

"No, ma'am. It was a pretty sunny morning all the way to town."

"Are you sure?"

"Yes, ma'am, I'm sure. I could feel the sun tanning my face." He grinned at her. His white teeth, bright against his dark skin.

The hat lady sputtered and her face turned red. "No need to be rude," she fumed at his back as he left.

He muttered, "Even if I did see a mist, I wouldn't tell her. She spreads gossip so fast, Hattie would know about it before I got home."

He stepped off the porch, rubbing his hand over his face.

CHAPTER 22

I t was close to noon. John Henry went back to the depot to pick up his picnic basket. Rusty sat on the seat of the buckboard, enjoying the sunshine. His tail tapped a few times when he saw his owner. Then he stood up and stretched, ready to go.

"Not yet, Rusty. You stay here and guard the wagon."

Rusty sat down with a heavy sigh and a groan.

"I know. I know. Just a little while longer. Okay, boy?"

The Flint River bank offered a quiet place where he could settle down and eat his lunch. The lunch Hattie had packed hit the spot. Smoked ham on homemade bread, a wedge of homemade cheese, an apple from the tree out back, and a jar of tea left over from breakfast.

He looked off to the west of the city. Something caught his eye. He sat up for a closer look. "Well, I'll be danged!" He shaded his eyes from the sun and squinted. "That looks like a gray mist," he mumbled.

Woooooooot! Wooooo! Wooooooot, screamed the 1:45 train as it announced its impending arrival into town.

"Can't worry about that now, I guess." He got up and made his way back to the depot.

CHAPTER 23

T he yard workers finished loading the wagon with iron. Once Ole Mule was hitched up, all that needed to be done was make a quick stop at Murphy's Mercantile to pick up Hattie's order.

John Henry smiled and gave a sigh of relief as he drove his buckboard out of town. "Ole Mule, are you as glad as I am to get out of that busy, noisy place?"

Ole Mule flicked his right ear and swished his tail.

"Yup, I feel the same way," laughed John Henry. "Get up, Mule. If we hurry, we might get home before dark."

Rusty, the redbone hound, shared the bench beside John Henry. He was almost asleep. His head hung over the edge of the bench seat. When the buckboard jiggled over the lumps on the two-track road, Rusty's head rocked to-and-fro. John Henry put his hand on the dog's head and gave him a pat.

A raven sat on the high branches of a tree by the trail. It cocked its head and watched the man and mule as they made their way west, toward the gully. *Caw! Caw!* it yelled at them. The raven watched their progress until they disappeared into the grove of trees. It launched itself into the air and flew out of sight.

The grove of trees was the halfway point to the farm. Ole Mule usually picked up speed at the gully with the dry wash. Today, however, Ole Mule slowed down to almost a stop.

"Well, what's wrong with you? It'll take us all night to get home at this speed."

John Henry smacked the driving lines across Ole Mule's rump to get his attention.

Mule came to a complete stop. Rusty sat up, blinked, and looked around.

"Come on, Mule, let's move. Get up."

His ears flicked forward then laid back on his head. His nose wrinkled. He flipped his head and stomped his foot, but he held his ground. Rusty jumped to his feet, looking in the same direction as Mule.

"*Ggggrrrr,*" came a low growl from the hound dog. His fur stood up from the top of his head to the tip of his tail.

"What do you see, boy?" John Henry took a closer look down in the gully. "I don't see anything. Why are you both having such a hissy fit? We got to go down there. It's the only way home."

He climbed down from the seat, walked up to Mule's head, and took a hold of the bridle.

"It's okay, boy. Nothing's gonna hurt you. Come on, just a little bit farther."

He tried to lead the mule down the path. After about three steps, Ole Mule refused to move.

Rusty jumped down from the seat. He sniffed the air, paced along the edge of the gully and gave another long, low, rumbling growl. "I ain't never seen you act so." He tied Ole Mule to a tree. "Sorry, boy, I know you'd like to eat this sweet grass, but I'm not going to chase you all over the county side should you take off. So stop tossing your head."

He turned and looked at Rusty. "Guard," he said as he pointed to Mule.

CHAPTER 24

J ohn Henry took off his beat-up old hat and scratched his head. He looked again at the bottom of the gully then glanced back at the animals.

What is wrong with those two crazy critters? he mumbled to himself. *Something must be powerfully wrong for Ole Mule not to want to go home. Better have me a look-see.*

He grabbed one of the iron rods out of the bed of the buckboard. Laying it over his shoulder like a rifle, he started down the hill. A grayish fog seemed to be settling over the dry wash. A raven yelled out a few times, but John Henry paid no attention.

About halfway down the hill, the sun no longer penetrated the fog. The leaves stopped rustling in the breeze, and the birds stopped singing. With each step he took, the fog got denser. He looked over his shoulder to check on Rusty and Ole Mule, but all he could see was the fog.

"Jooohhhnnn," came a hissing whisper from the trees.

With a death grip on the iron, he said, "Who's there? Who said that? What do you want?"

In front of him, the path began to crack and shatter into millions of pieces. The pieces turned and curled, yet they didn't collapse into a heap on the ground, like a broken mirror.

He shook his head, rubbed his eyes, and took another look, as two strangers materialized out of the swirling mass. In a strained voice, Lisa and App heard him say, "What in the Sam Hill is going on?"

The mist took advantage of the distraction. It became denser and darker. It seeped out of the underbrush and swirled toward John Henry's feet. It snaked about his legs and inched up his body undetected. At the last minute, it tightened like a rope and pined his arms to his sides.

John Henry pulled his eyes away from the strangers on the road in front of him and looked down at his body, wrapped in the evil mist of a rope. "*Aaahhh!*" he roared. He wiggled and struggled to break free, but nothing worked.

The souls of the tortured dead rolled and twisted in the misty haze that danced around him. Empty eye sockets stared out at him as they whirled past. Silent screams were frozen on their faces. Boney hands reached out to touch him and draw him into their evil realm of darkness.

"John Henry," they called in unison. "We want to be your friend. Come with us, and you can be rich and famous. Imagine the fine house and beautiful dresses you can give your wife. She will be happier than she has ever been. You can be richer than your wildest dreams," hissed the sinister mist.

John Henry stopped struggling, and his eyes took on a glassy haze as the mist hypnotized him.

CHAPTER 25

L isa and App stepped into the year 1870 to find a huge man tangled in the vines of the evil mist.

Lisa shed her backpack.

App asked, "What do you think you are doing?"

"Give me the salt. I'm going to confront the demon. We have faced off before. I'm going to stop this. Hurry up! Give me the salt." She exchanged the holy water for the salt.

App grabbed her arm.

"Let me go. I have to do this. That is why we are here. I'll be okay, but we have to hurry before the man gives in or gives up."

The darkness spun around like a whirlwind. It emitted a piercing hiss that deafened the ears. It wound around its victim tighter and tighter.

"My dear friend, all you have to do is ask us to come in. Just relax and open your mind," the mist whispered to John Henry.

Lisa marched up the edge of the disturbance, took a deep breath, and screamed, *"Let him go!"* She moved closer. "Evil darkness, I command you to let him go." She flung salt on the demon.

It hissed, rolled, and pulled away from the salt. Its loops loosened and slid down John Henry's body and lay in coils at his feet.

Lisa addressed the man, "Mister, you must listen to me. If you don't drive away the darkness now, it will continue to follow you. If it can't get to you, it will go after your family. Do you understand what I am saying to you? Mister, you must banish it *now!*"

App had worked his way around to the other side. He crept unnoticed as close as he possibly could. He held the jar of holy water, ready to toss it into the mist.

John Henry's eyes cleared of the glassy haze, and he raged like a beast, "*No*, not me or my family."

At the same time, Lisa emptied the box of salt on the vile, dark mist, and App opened the jar of holy water and splattered the coils. The darkness, with its tortured souls, dissolved to ash and blew away in an instant.

Overhead, a raven circled and yelled out its annoying call and landed on a tree not too far away. It waited and watched.

CHAPTER 26

The sound of his master's voice brought Rusty on the run. He charged down the gully at full speed. "Bowwwww. Bowwwww," his deep baying voice echoed through the gully. Under thorny shrubs and over fallen trees, he scurried. Rusty entered the clearing and ran past his master and placed himself between his master and the two strangers. The giant of a man stood with the iron at his shoulder, ready to swing at Lisa and App.

"Dog, get away from them."

"Grrrrr" was followed by a whine.

John Henry yelled at the dog, "Rusty, I don't want to hit you! Now move."

Rusty reared up on his hind feet and stood in front of Lisa and App, facing John Henry.

Slowly, the iron rod slid off his shoulder, and he looked at the dog and the strangers standing behind him. Rusty went down in a belly crawl and wormed his way over to John Henry. He rolled over onto his back and gave a soft whine.

"Well, I be danged." He studied his dog and then studied the two odd-looking visitors dressed in blue jeans, T-shirts, and nylon jackets.

The huge man rubbed his face. "If Rusty trusts you, then I guess I should too. My name is John Henry Steel," he said as he offered his hand. "Who are you, and why are you dressed so strange?"

CHAPTER 27

Three hours later, the buckboard pulled into the yard. Hattie ran out on the porch. "Land's sake, man, where have you been? I thought you would be home before…"

Hattie drew up short when she saw the visitors. She wiped her hands on the apron and tucked her hair back under her scarf. "Welcome to our humble home. Please come in and make yourselves comfortable."

"I bet y'all are starving, aren't ya? Have a seat at the table, and you can warm up with a bowl of stew," said Hattie as she dished up a bowl for each of them.

"Sweet Pea, my new friends here saved my life," began John Henry.

"Don't go spinning no tale, you silly ox." Hattie laughed and placed a fresh pan of johnnycake on the table. "More like you picked up a tree and scared a bear away, saving their lives."

The room was quiet except for the snapping and popping of the wood in the fireplace. Laugher left her eyes as she studied the faces of the three at the table.

With her hands in fists and resting on her hips, she said, "Well, maybe someone better tell me what happened."

"Sweet Pea, I think you better sit down for this."

He patted the bench beside him. Once she was seated, he put his arm around her and kissed her cheek. Then for the next several hours, John Henry, Lisa, and App did their best to describe what happened.

"I can't say I believe everything that you have said," stated Hattie. "But I do believe there is evil in this world. I believe it does take control of people. We face temptation every day. That much I do believe. So for now let's leave it at that. It is late. If you want to go see Miss Mackie tomorrow, you'll need to get some rest."

CHAPTER 28

App helped hook Ole Mule to the buckboard early the next morning.

"I'll take you to town and show ya where the hospital is. But I can't go in with you. I guess you knows that. Colored people are not allowed in, lest they work there."

Hattie and Lisa walked out onto the porch. Lisa stepped forward in a long calico-print skirt and white blouse. She looked like she had stepped out of a history book.

App turned from hooking a trace to the whippletree and stared at her. "Why are you dressed like that?"

Hattie answered in a matter-of-fact voice, "Young man, girls can't run around in trousers. It just isn't done. You can't tell everyone you are from the future. They won't believe you. I can't say as I do either. You'd be sent to an asylum for the insane. It's better to have you look like poor folks."

"Hattie, I don't look like poor folk."

Lisa studied the clothes. They were handmade, with a bit of lace for decoration.

"I'm thinking that these might be your best clothes. They are, aren't they?"

"Well," Hattie said, "That is my Sunday go-to-meeting dress. But I can't send you off to town in a ragged work dress now, can I?"

John Henry smile and said, "Miss Lisa, you look right nice in that dress. Just as pretty as my Hattie."

"Thank you, that was nice of you to say."

"You need to get going. It will be noon before you get to town at this speed." Hattie shooed them on their way.

CHAPTER 29

“I'm sorry, mister—ah—what did you say your name was?” inquired the nurse.

“App. My name is App.”

“Most unusual name indeed. It's like this, Mr. App, you are not a family member, so you are not allowed in the woman's wing. Do I make myself clear?” The nurse stood in the door, blocking the way.

“May I go and talk to Miss Mackie?” asked Lisa.

“She is supposed to be resting. She has serious burns,” warned the nurse.

“I promise, I won't stay long. We have come a long way to see her.”

The nurse looked Lisa over. “Okay, young lady. You may go in alone, but you can only stay five minutes.”

“Thank you so much.”

“She is in bed number eight in the far-right corner.”

The room was crowded. Each bed had a small table beside it and was sectioned off by a rolling screen for privacy. Lisa walked quietly past the other patients. She stopped at the foot of Miss Mackie's bed and paused a moment.

Miss Mackie's face and eyes were wrapped in white bandages. Her right hand was also bound. “Are you going to stand there and stare all day?”

“No, ma'am. I thought you might be asleep and didn't want to wake you.”

"I'm awake. Who are you? I don't recognize your voice."

"I'm Lisa."

"Miss Lisa, huh. If you are a reporter, I have nothing to say." Miss Mackie fussed with the blankets with her good hand and wiggled around in the bed.

"No, ma'am, I'm not a reporter. But I do need to ask you what caused the fire. Yesterday, my friend and I had an encounter with an evil black mist and—"

Miss Mackie froze. She tilted her head at a slight angle. She was completely focused. "This time, give me the real answer. *Who* are *you?*"

"I don't have time to explain everything. I came to restrict the evil mist's interaction with people."

Miss Mackie sat straight up in bed with agitated movements. "Stay away from the mist. It'll hurt you."

"Please, stay calm. It's okay. I've had encounters with it before. Last evening, when it attacked John Henry, my friend, App and I were able to extinguish it."

Miss Mackie laid back against the pillow. "You're more than what you seem, aren't you, Miss Lisa? Okay, this is what happened. Webster is a big kid, but dad is bigger. I think his dad is abusive. He came into school with two shiners, and he wouldn't sit down on the hard benches."

"Did he come to school with bruises a lot?"

"Yes, and on this day, one of the little kids, Jamie, teased him. He had a bad temper. I began walking toward him when I caught a glimpse of movement outside the window. A gray-colored mist oozed out of the trees and rapidly advanced toward the school. The next thing I knew, it was squeezing up between the floor boards." Miss Mackie shivered.

"Are you okay?" Lisa said as she took a step closer to the bed.

"It makes my skin crawl the way it circled the classroom. Like bony hands, it grabbed Webster's feet. His eyes glazed over, and he walked to the stove. Without any hesitation, he opened the potbellied stove door and reached in with bare hands. He grabbed a burning log and went after Jamie first. When he missed him, he swung the burning log at the other students and then the furniture. The charred wood broke up and sent chunks of red-hot coals all over the room. In a blink of an eye, the school was on fire."

"What did you do?"

"I got the older girls to help the younger children out of the building. Then I held Webster's attention while the rest of the students ran out. I tried to get him to come outside with me, but it was too late. That is when I got burned."

The floorboards of the hospital room squeaked as the nurse walked up.

"Time is up. You will have to leave. You have upset Miss Mackie."

Lisa hesitated a moment and then said to Miss Mackie, "Something tells me that you're more than you seem too. I'll see you in the future, won't I?"

"You certainly will, my dear. I'll look forward to it."

"You need to leave now," stressed the nurse.

Lisa reached out and took Miss Mackie's unbandage hand. "Until then," she said and walked away.

App met Lisa at the door. "Did you get what you needed?"

"I sure did. Let's find John Henry. It's time to go home."

CHAPTER 30

G and Miss Pinky had not walked more than a dozen feet when they heard a soft sound behind them. They spun around in time to see Lisa and App step through the shattered crystals of time.

"Why are you back so soon? Is everything all right?" gushed Miss Pinky as she hustled over to them.

"Everything went better than we could have planned," said App.

"But you have only been gone a few minutes," stated G-Master.

"We were gone for two days. I just chose to come back close to the same time as we left," Lisa explained.

"Of course you did. I forget how good you are at time travel, you clever girl. Let's get home. Pinky and I can hardly wait to hear about your adventure."

They arrived home and gathered in the dining room. Lisa and App told their story over several cups of hot chocolate.

G and Pinky studied the young people seated at the table with them. "Well done, well done," he said. "I have to admit, you handled yourselves better than most adults would under those scary circumstances. You two make an excellent team."

"It's good to know that 1870 isn't where we need to focus our attention," added Miss Pinky.

"I agree," declared Lisa. "Now we have to make plans for the future."

CHAPTER 31

*One week, two days, and one hour
until the time glitches collide.*

They checked supplies, made some adjustments, and, with
packs on their backs, they were ready for their journey to
October 30, 2170.

"All this time-travel stuff makes me a nervous wreck," Pinky
confessed. She took in a deep, shaky breath.

G moved up next to his wife and put his arm around her. He
took his glasses off and rubbed the bridge of his nose. He stood still
for a second, with his eyes closed. He gave a heavy sigh, placed his
glasses back on his nose, and then shared a serious look with Lisa
and App. "I just want to caution you that going forward in time is
more dangerous than going back. There are no written records to
which you can refer and no idea of who the good guys are or who
you can trust. It is with great reservation that I agree to let you take
this trip."

"It's okay, G. I know that if you had a choice, you would not
let us go. We both understand that, at the very least, this is a risky
venture. This is my task; it is what I was selected to do. I will do it to
the best of my ability," vowed Lisa.

App smiled at the small group of people gathered in front of the school. "Aw, come on now, you guys. It is not going to be that bad. You forget I have seen Lisa in action. I know we're going to be fine."

"That's right," said Lisa. "We are going to be fine. We will be back here faster than you can do a tap dance."

CHAPTER 32

Taking App's hand, Lisa stepped off the school's steps, into the future. They stumbled into an overgrown field of long grass, weeds, and shrubs.

Safety being the first concern, they took cover so they could investigate their surroundings without being seen. Birds chirped, bugs buzzed, and the breeze softly rustled the grass and the leaves around them. However, there were no people, cars, or buildings of any kind. There was nothing that appeared to be of any great danger.

"All seems to be clear," commented App.

"Something doesn't feel quite right. I don't know what it is, but there is a disturbance of some kind. I think it is coming from..." said Lisa as she slowly turned in a circle. "Yes, there it is. It seems to be coming from that way." Lisa pointed in the direction of a cluster of pine trees.

"Let's find a place to stash these packs."

"Good idea."

They shed their large packs and withdrew a pair of binoculars and a pocketknife.

"That clump of bushes is a great place to hide our backpacks." App pointed to a scrubby group of shrubs. "Once covered with the camo tarp, the packs will be invisible."

When that chore was completed, they followed the direction of the disturbance. They wandered only a few yards when App tripped over a chunk of rocks stuck together. He picked it up to study it. "What the heck is this?"

Lisa looked at the item in his hand and then explored the ground. "Well, I'll be darned. That, my friend, is very old concrete. I believe you are holding a piece of the old school building or parking lot. Look over here," she said as she walked a few more steps. "Here is where the old asphalt road connected to the parking lot."

App scrunched his forehead into wrinkles as he walked past her. "If that were true, then what are the cars driving on? That must mean that, in this year, they don't use cars."

"More importantly, this must be our neighborhood. Where are all the people and houses?" asked Lisa.

"Oh, yeah. Right."

"Let's go. I still feel a disturbance this way."

The longer they walked, the stronger the feeling of disturbance and irritation became.

In the distance, they could see some kind of structure. Lisa and App eased toward the building. Long grass and brush were the perfect cover. They slid under a small bush about fifty yards from the building. App took out his binoculars, laid on his belly, and studied the structure.

"I think it is a house. What do you think?" he said as he handed the binoculars to Lisa.

She wormed down under the bush beside him and focused on the building. "I believe you are right. But it's awful large for one family, isn't it?"

"I'd say you're correct on that."

"How're we going to know who to observe?"

"The feeling of annoyance and anger is overwhelming. It is getting stronger as we speak. Let's wait a few minutes and see what happens."

It didn't take long.

CHAPTER 33

"*Caw. Caw. Caw*," called the black raven as it landed on a twig that looked too small to support its weight.

"*Caw. Caw*," came an answer from a long way off.

He fluffed his long neck feathers, shook his head, flicked his wings once or twice, and answered his friend. A breeze blew, and he bounced around as the twig blew in the wind, but he didn't move. He appeared to be waiting.

Not far from his perch was the multifamily geodome living unit. A door swung open with a bang, out stormed a seven-year-old girl. She turned, looked back at the door, and waited a moment.

"You lied to me! You told me you would take me to the zoo. It was my idea. You promised. Now you want to take your fancy-pants girlfriend, and I can't go." She leaned slightly at the waist toward the door and screamed in a singsong voice, "I can't hear you!" Then she kicked the door.

Her brother's footsteps grew louder as they neared the door. The curly-headed girl jumped out of the way as the door banged open.

"Can you hear me now?" bellowed the teenager. "I don't care if the zoo was your idea. I want to spend time with my girlfriend."

"You mean Miss Fancy Pants?" she mocked.

"I told you, stop calling her that."

"Fancy Pants, Fancy Pants."

"You call her that one more time, I'll—"

"You'll what?" she dared.

"I'll slap you."

"Fancy Pants, Fancy Pants."

He flew off the porch swifter than a hornet protecting its nest. His hand slapped her across the face so fast, they both froze. He had left a perfect hand-shaped mark on her cheek.

His eyes widened. He looked at her face and then at his hand. Slowly, he extended a hand toward her red cheek.

"Jazzy, I am so sorry. I didn't mean to do that."

She stared at her brother. Her eyes turned red, and tears shimmered at the edges but didn't spill over. "*I hate you*," she spit out the words at him as though they left a foul taste in her mouth. "What kind of a brother are you?" growled the girl through clinched teeth.

He retreated a few steps, turned, and slunk back into the house, letting the door slam. She remained frozen until she heard the personal transport unit start up. In just seconds, the PTU lifted off. As it passed overhead, the displaced air from the thrusters blew her curls into her eyes. She pushed her hair back, and she stuck her tongue out at him.

The tears that had rimmed in her eyes earlier now streamed down her face. What to do now seemed to hang in the air. With a large inhale of breath, the girl ran into the house.

CHAPTER 34

As if on cue, the evil mist appeared. It slowly lifted from the weeds and grasses, like a thin wisp of white smoke. It hung a scant eighth of an inch above the growth.

Minutes later, the door opened again. Jazzy carried a pack on her back, a water bottle under one arm, and a lumpy pillowcase under the other. Not bothering to look back at the living unit, she stepped off the porch and started walking through the weeds and small brush. The mist swirled around her feet as she went.

"*Caw. Caw. Caw,*" called the raven.

"Black-Jack, I don't have time to play today. I'm leaving."

"*Trp, trp, trp,*" mumbled Black-Jack.

"Don't try to stop me."

The raven ruffled his neck feathers and eyed the lumpy pillowcase she carried. He flew a few yards ahead of her, landed, and hopped toward her. "Want some. Want some. Want some."

"I already told you, I don't have time for games, Black-Jack."

Not taking no for an answer, Black-Jack walked right up to Jazzy and, with a sharp, pointed beak, he pecked a hole in the lumpy bag.

"Stop that. I told you no!" she shouted as she swung the bag away from Black-Jack.

Jazzy stomped her foot at the raven. Black-Jack backed off a bit then scolded her with a loud caw as he launched into the air. After circling once, he headed toward a mega-giant oak tree in the far-off distance.

"Stupid bird. I told you I didn't have time to play!"

She kicked a rock and walked away from her home, lugging her treasures with her.

The wispy smoke collected itself as it drifted in behind her, but it kept its distance.

CHAPTER 35

"Bingo," whispered Lisa as she watched the wisps of smoke follow the girl. "I didn't see the mist until she started to walk in the grass. See, it's right there, above the grass." She handed the binoculars back to App.

He searched the area. "Where? I don't see it."

"I'd guess it is about two yards behind her, and it is very light, almost white and transparent. It hasn't dredged up a frenzy yet. But you can bet it is working on it," commented Lisa.

He scanned the area behind Jazzy. "Aaahhhh, yes. I see it now. The girl's aura is very dark and swirling, like a tornado. Evil may have a good chance of influencing her. I do believe we have found the cause of the disturbance."

They followed her at a distance to the oak tree. In a dense cluster of bushes just a few yards away, they found a place where they could watch her and remain undetected.

"I think you should try to talk to her," suggested App.

Thoughtfully, Lisa shared, "If she can face this challenge alone and win, she will be a stronger person."

"But what if the evil tries to overpower her?"

"We're close enough, we can help if she needs us. I have a feeling she can take care of herself."

Quietly, they settled down in the grass under the shrubs and watched.

"You have the binoculars," said Lisa. "Why don't you take first watch."

CHAPTER 36

The oak had stood guard over what once had been Burton for at about one hundred and sixty years. It had long limbs that swept low to the ground and then skyward. It offered a place to hide to anyone who needed to run away.

Jazzy ran up to the tree, dropped her treasures, and hugged it. Her sobs could be heard across the meadow.

"Granddad, I hate my brother. He lied to me. He has been promising me a trip to the zoo for a month. Now he has gone without me. You are the only one I can depend on," sniffed Jazzy. Her tears fell onto Granddad's bark.

Jazzy wiped her nose on her sleeve. She stooped and gathered up her items then climbed up into Granddad's branches. She found her favorite perch and made herself at home.

The mist collected around the base of the tree. It swirled around, like a hound sniffing out a rabbit. Then it settled down.

Jazzy sat on the tree branch, leaning her body against Granddad's wide trunk. One knee was bent with her foot resting on the branch, and the other foot was swinging in agitation.

"Someday, when I am big enough, I will get even with him. I will hurt his feelings then I will leave him to be all alone. Just wait and see. He will be sorry."

The mist swirled and turned into a vine. The vine crept up the tree. It looked like a time-lapse film; it grew so fast. Once it had wrapped around the trunk of the tree, it spread onto the branch on which Jazzy sat. She shuffled her foot a bit as it eased up to her.

"Helloooo," it hissed to Jazzy. "Is there anything I can do to help? Getting even with someone is one of my specialties. I can make your brother wish he had never been born."

"*Caw, Caw, Caw,*" yelled Black-Jack as he landed on one of Granddad's upper branches. He turned his head and eyed the vine closely. With a flick of his wings he landed on Jazzy's foot. "Love you," he said. "Love you." He jumped down on the branch then hopped over to the vine and pecked it.

"*Hissssssss*, go away you ugly bird," sassed the devilish vine.

"Love you," repeated Black-Jack. Again, the raven took a vicious peck at the vine.

"Ouch! Stop that," the vine hissed. It curled away from the raven.

Black-Jack studied the vine closely, blinked a time or two, hopped closer, and jabbed it one more time. This time, he removed a chunk of bark.

"*Aggggh,*" roared the evil vine. It curled up into a loop and knocked Black-Jack off the branch.

"Black-Jack, are you okay? Don't you dare hurt my bird. I love him," cried Jazzy.

Jazzy pulled out a miniature souvenir Detroit Tiger's baseball bat from the pillowcase and took to whaling on the vine.

The vine shriveled at the word "love." It hardly had time to recover when it was hit.

"Don't you ever hurt someone I love, you horrible, wicked thing."

Jazzy beat the vine flat in several places and began stripping leaves off it. The vine tried to pull away, but she was standing on it. Given no chance to escape as a vine, it changed back into a mist and disappeared."

"Don't you ever come back here again. You hear me?" hollered Jazzy. "Black-Jack. Here, Black-Jack. Where are you?"

"*Caw-Caw,*" came the answer as he made his way through the branches. "Want some. Want some."

"Of course you do, you clever bird," soothed Jazzy.

She dug around in the pillowcase and pulled out some jerky. She broke off a hunk and handed it to Black-Jack then took a bite for herself. They sat on Granddad's branches and munched on their treat.

CHAPTER 37

"Holy cow! Did you see that?" App struggled to keep his voice at a whisper. "She just beat the living daylights out of the vine. You were right to let her handle it herself."

"But remember what happened when she said she loved Black-Jack?"

"Ooohhh, umm, well…the vine jumped. It jumped even before she took to beating on it. Why? Is that important?"

"Maybe."

"Jaaazzy, Jazzzzzzzzzy, Jazzy, where are you, kiddo?" called her brother as he walked toward Granddad.

"No one here by that name," she called back. She made no attempt to climb down.

"Then who am I talking to?"

"Don't know. Don't care."

He made it across the field and stood under Granddad. He shaded his eyes from the sun and looked up at her through the leaves.

"I want to talk to you. Why not come down?"

"Nope."

"Your brother wants to say he's sorry."

"Don't have a brother."

"Yes, you do. I'm right here."

"Nope. A real brother would not lie, slap his sister, and take off with Fancy Pants."

78

With a heavy sigh, he said, "That's what I want to talk to you about."

"Nope, I ain't comin' down."

"You leave me no choice. I'm comin' up." He shimmed up the tree as fast as Jazzy had.

"How'd you find me?"

"Who showed you this tree in the first place and taught you how to climb it, silly? Your brother."

Jazzy turned her back to him. "That couldn't be me. I don't have a brother."

"Aw, come on, Jazzy. I said I'm sorry." He hung his head. "Would it make you feel any better if I told you that you are right?"

Jazzy shifted on the branch a bit and looked over her shoulder at him. "It might."

"We hadn't gone far when my PTU lost lift and we were stuck. Buck saw us and stopped. He had his brand-new, super-sport model with the swanky flames. Fancy Pants jumped in his vehicle and was gone before I knew what happened."

He snatched a leaf off the branch closest to him. As he talked, he shredded it and threw the pieces on the ground.

He shook his head, and with a heavy sigh, said, "Man, she didn't even look back."

They sat for a moment in silence.

"I am so sorry. I didn't want to think that she was usin' me even though deep down, I knew she was. I really would rather spend time sittin' in this tree with you than go out with the likes of her. What do you say, Jazzy? Will you accept my apology?"

She had shifted around to face her brother. "Don't you ever let it happen again." Jazzy whacked him in the arm.

"Ouch!" He rubbed his arm. "That is one wicked punch you got there. Where did you learn to do that?"

"My brother taught me."

"He must be one cool brother."

"Yeah, but sometimes he's a fool."

"Sure, sometimes brothers are fools. That's why they need little sisters to keep them in line. Listen, Jazzy, I can't say I won't ever have another girlfriend. But I'll make this promise, I won't let anyone spoil any plans we make together, and I'll never ever hit you again."

"You better not." She dug around in the pillowcase and pulled out a package of jerky. She handed a stick to him. "Would you like some?"

"Wow, that's my favorite kind." He raised it to his mouth to take a bite. Black-Jack swooped down out of the branches. "Want some, want some." The raven landed on his arm long enough to snatch the jerky out of his hand and fly away.

"You stupid black bird, come back here with that. It's mine."

Jazzy laughed until she couldn't breathe.

Lisa and App wiggled out from under the bushes and slipped way. A single rainbow sprinkle landed on Lisa's cheek. Ever so softly, she heard the voice of the Wise One in her ear.

"Well done, Lisa. Your wisdom is beyond your years." As the voice faded, so did the sprinkle.

App turned and looked back at Lisa. She jogged a bit to catch up with him.

"Is everything okay?"

"Yup, everything is just fine. The disturbance in 2170 has disappeared, and it is time to get back to 2020," she answered as she playfully punched him on the shoulder before she took off running.

"Hey. Wait for me," he called as they went to retrieve their packs and go home.

CHAPTER 38

L isa and App had stepped into the future. G-Master scanned the area around the school. He gave Pinky a silly little smirk, pulled his glasses down on his nose, old-grandpa style, and he started to click his heel. He shuffled forward and back and grabbed Pinky for a swing.

"For goodness sakes, what do you think you are doing?" asked Pinky.

"What does it look like I'm doing?"

"You silly man, you look like you are dancing."

"And so I am."

"Whatever for?"

"You heard Lisa. She said that they would be back before we stopped tap dancing. I don't know how to tap dance, but I can sure spin you around the dance floor. Come on, gal, kick up your heels."

"G, sometimes you are just too silly." She danced with him in the darkness.

Behind them, two preteens stepped through the crystal portal. They stood for a moment and watched the couple dance. As they slowed, Pinky's magical laugh filled the air.

"What are you doing?" asked App.

"Lisa told us to tap dance. We don't know how, so we are making it up as we go," G said.

Bark. Bark. Bark.

A large, black dog across the street ran up to the fence and announced to the world that intruders were out and about. The pit bull two doors down joined in the chorus, followed by the three dogs on the next block.

Giving G a push from behind, Pinky grabbed Lisa's hand and then App's. Pinky directed everyone toward the car. "Come on, we need to get out of here. The neighborhood dogs are starting to make a fuss."

CHAPTER 39

On Monday morning, the sky was gray. The rain started as a soft mist, but by the time they left for school, it had begun to pour down. As the rain increased, so did the wind.

Lisa fought the wind with her umbrella and walked without comment. App, on the other hand, held nothing back. He complained as soon as they had left the house. His rain slicker flipped in the wind and slapped him in the face. He wiped the water away for the third time.

"I don't know why I couldn't drive the car today. G and Pinky don't need the car. This is ridiculous, walking in the rain," he objected.

"Don't be silly. You're too young to drive the car."

"No, I'm not. I have been driving since I was seven back on Time Island. In fact, this year, I can apply for my heavy-equipment license."

"Hate to be the one to have to tell you, this is not Time Island. The law here says you must be sixteen before you can drive."

"Well, it is a stupid law." He continued to grumble as he stomped in a puddle. Muddy water splashed in all directions.

The wind caught his slicker again and sent cold rainwater onto his face.

"Doggone it," he sputtered as he wiped away the rain.

"Oh my goodness, you are such a big baby. One minute you are all serious and acting like an adult, and now you're acting like a two-year-old. I wouldn't let you drive either if I saw you acting like this." She snickered and elbowed him in the ribs.

His frown turned into a smirk, "Yeah, I know. I guess I have to agree with you. But treat me like a child, I will act like a child. Treat me like an adult, I will act like an adult."

"Cheer up," she replied. "I can see the school. We are almost there."

CHAPTER 40

M r. Zornet stood at the landing in the big window of the school. He watched the students. He paced back and forth like a caged animal. He stopped, scanned the sidewalk, and paced some more.

"Hey, Zornet," said the coach after he had observed Z's behavior for several moments. "What are you doing, waiting for the promotion to department head? Nope, that can't be it. That was announced last month. Let's see who got that position. Oh, that's right, it was me. Better luck next time, buddy. Haw haw hee hee." The coach snorted as he turned his back and walked away.

Zornet's face turned three shades of red. "We will see who's laughing when everything is all said and done." He turned his attention back to the sidewalk. It was clogged with wet students as they awaited the bell. Lisa and App had just joined the line and huddled under the umbrella.

Zornet heard the door open downstairs. Then the most amazing thing happened. Zornet gripped the railing and leaned closer to the window as if that would help him see and hear what took place below. His mouth dropped open, and his eyes grew wide.

CHAPTER 41

Lisa and App stood in line as they waited for the bell to ring. Rain dripped off the umbrella and ran down App's neck. Lisa could still hear him grumbling that he should have been able to drive to school. She giggled and jabbed him again.

With a resounding bang, the steel school door swung open and hit the wall. Out stepped Miss Mackie. She marched toward Lisa. The students on the sidewalk parted before her, as the sea parted for Moses.

At the end of her march, she stood face to face with Lisa.

"You are the one, are you not?"

Lisa took a deep breath and squared her shoulders. Eye to eye with Miss Mackie, she said, "Yes, I do believe I am."

"I thought so." Miss Mackie begun to turn away.

"And you," stated Lisa, "are not as you seem, are you?"

"That would also be true," she replied with a nod as she marched to the door. Once at the door, she opened it then twisted back to Lisa and said, "We shall talk more later."

Miss Mackie disappeared into the mouth of the school. The door slammed shut behind her.

The students held their positions as they watched the exchange. The bell sounded, and they still didn't move. Arthur and his posse pushed to the front of the crowd and hustled up to Lisa and App. The misfits shared a fist bump and fell in behind Lisa and App as they walked toward the door. Just like that, they went from nobodies to friends of someone special.

Up on the landing, Mr. Zornet paced and rubbed his hands together. "Something is going to happen soon."

CHAPTER 42

That evening, G, Pinky, Lisa, and App sat around the table. Pinky had a beef roast with potatoes and homemade biscuits. G had just scooped up a big forkful and was ready to chow down when the doorbell rang.

"Are we expecting someone?" he asked.

"No one that I know of," said Pinky.

Bing-bong, rang the bell again.

"I'll get it," said App as he stood up and walked to the door.

Bing-bong. The bell rang a third time.

App opened the door, and there stood Miss Mackie. She wore a floor-length, charcoal-gray cape with a loose hood. It was lined with red satin. She looked every bit the part of a witch, as Mr. Zornet said she was.

"Took you long enough to open the door," stated Miss Mackie as she walked past App and marched into the dining room.

She swirled her cape off and tossed it at App. It hit him on the top of his head. He snatched it off his head and frowned as he wiped water off his face.

"Oh, great. More rain water, just what I needed," he muttered as he placed the cape on the chair by the heater to let it dry. Miss Mackie sat down in App's chair.

"Let's get this out of the way first. No one here is as they seem. I figure you three," she said as she pointed to G, Pinky, and App, "are some kind of time keepers or watchers. Is that true?" she asked.

G and Pinky replied at the same time, "Yes."

"As I thought. But you, Miss Lisa, you are far more than that. It has taken me a long while to fit the pieces together. The incident with the kickball and the visit to the hospital helped to finish the puzzle. You, my dear, are royalty of the Old Order. You have no idea of your capabilities. You are extraordinary right now, but, in the future, you will be very powerful. Right now you are learning in little steps, as you should be."

She looked at Pinky and G. "You are doing a fine job teaching her."

"In truth," confessed Pinky, "she is teaching us."

"Ah, yes, I can believe that," Miss Mackie gave a wispy smile.

Lisa interrupted, "What about you, Miss Mackie?"

She gave a heavy sigh. "I'm but a humble servant that has just about completed my mission. I'm ready for a long-deserved rest. Let us not speak of it anymore. Yum, this roast smells great. I wouldn't mind if I had some."

The family shared a surprised look.

"Please, Miss Mackie. Help yourself. App, get another chair, and Lisa, get another plate," said Pinky. "Would you like tea or hot chocolate?"

"Hot tea sounds lovely."

Once everyone was comfortable, they began their meal for the second time. The kitchen was filled with the sounds of a family sharing a meal—forks scraping the plates, cups being placed back on the table, and items being passed around the table as people asked for second servings. G took a big scoop of gravy-smothered biscuits. "Mmmm! This is the best meal ever," he said as he savored the beefy rich flavor.

Miss Mackie interrupted the homey sounds of supper. "I guess you are wondering why I am here. I figure that you are planning for the big event. I thought you could use my help."

G swallowed his last bite and said, "Uhhhh, yes, we were working on a plan. But we don't have enough help to carry it out. I believe we need to bring in backup help."

"G, I have been thinking," interrupted Lisa. "We don't have time to bring help from home. It would take too long to teach them everything they need to know to blend in. Why don't we get help from the kids at school? I know Arthur would jump at the chance to be included. I'm sure that Blossom, Pepper, Stinky, and Carlos will be willing to help if we ask."

"You have a point about outside help. But I'm not sure about involving locals," observed G.

"Oh, hogwash. If you were not here, don't you think that the locals would be involved?" asked Miss Mackie.

"I suppose that is true. But how would we explain things to them?"

Lisa interrupted, "We don't. We tell them that this is a top-secret Homeland Security mission. Information is given on a need-to-know basis. We tell them what their job will be and nothing more."

"What a great idea," added App. "I think they will buy it."

"I would like to add two more names to the list, Spooky and Bull," commented Miss Mackie.

"Bull, he tried to kill us. Why would we want to add him?" asked App with concern in his voice.

"Was Bull acting on his own, or was an outside force pushing him?"

"I believe," remarked Lisa, "he was angry, and an outside force manipulated him."

"That is what I thought too," replied Miss Mackie.

"Now, wait a minute," Pinky interrupted the conversation. "How do we know that it won't influence him again?"

With a thoughtful look on her face, Miss Mackie said, "He has been very humble since his return. I believe this will give him a chance to rebuild faith in himself and the trust of others."

App wrinkled his nose, "Okay, I can buy that, I guess. But why Spooky? She isn't very nice to me, and she tried to intimidate Lisa."

"Ah, Spooky," said Miss Mackie. "She is trying to find a way to fit in. This will be good for her too."

"Miss Mackie, do we need to be worried about Mr. Zornet?" inquired Lisa. "I get strange vibes when he is around. I feel like he is stalking me although he always has a reasonable excuse for being close by. I can't put my finger on it, but it just doesn't feel right."

Miss Mackie's face crinkled, and she stared Lisa in the eyes, "He is a slimy little worm, isn't he? He is so insignificant that he seems to be invisible. He is looking for anything that will make him notice-able. Don't take anything he says or does at face value. There is always an angle with him. When it is time to make a plan of action, we will find a way to neutralize his interference."

Miss Mackie then turned to Pinky and said, "This was a fine meal, Miss Pinky, but it is time I take my leave." Back to Lisa and App, she said, "We will meet tomorrow, after school, in my class-room. I will let Bull and Spooky know that their services are needed, and you two can contact the rest. Good night to all of you." Miss Mackie stood up, snatched up her dry cape, swirled it around her shoulders, and disappeared out the front door.

G-Master scratched his head. "Well, that was one interesting visit, wasn't it?"

CHAPTER 43

Three days and one hour until the timeline collision.

After school dismissed the next day, Miss Mackie prepared the room for the meeting. She moved the desks to form a semicircle. At 3:05, Lisa and App arrived.

"Do you think they will come?" Lisa asked Miss Mackie.

She answered the question with a question. "Why wouldn't they?"

Miss Mackie seemed confident, but Lisa watched the clock, paced a bit, and checked the clock again. Ten minutes after three, and still, no one showed. She sent a nervous look at App. He simply shrugged his shoulders.

Spooky was the first to arrive at 3:12. She looked at the seating arrangement, then walked to the back of the room and leaned against the wall. She folded her arms and glared at Lisa and App.

"I see Miss Congeniality has arrived," whispered App to Lisa.

There was a commotion in the hall. Miss Mackie went to the door. Mr. Zornet had stopped the rest of the students at the fire door.

"Just where do you think you are going?" he demanded of the students.

Arthur tried to explain. "We have an appointment with Miss Mackie, sir."

"All of you? That seems very unlikely?" Zornet inspected them like insects.

Blossom wrung her hands and said, "If we don't get to her room soon, she will think that we are not coming,"

"Your explanation is unacceptable. You need a better story than that if you want to go through these doors," he said with great authority.

"Mr. Zornet," interrupted Miss Mackie. "I'm glad I found you. Mr. Teeterman has been looking for you. He said there was some mix up in the selection of the new department head or something like that. He needs to see you by the end of today, or it will be too late."

Mr. Zornet spun around to face Miss Mackie. "Are you sure?"

"Yeah, he said something like that," she confirmed.

Mr. Zornet pushed past the students that he had been interrogating and rushed toward the office.

The students walked into Mackie's classroom.

"But, Miss Mackie, Mr. Teeterman left at lunchtime for a principal's meeting," Arthur announced.

Mackie smirked, "I know. Too bad Mr. Zornet won't catch up with him by the end of the day."

It took a moment for the students to understand, then they shared in the amusement.

Miss Mackie looked at the odd collection of students. "We have important matters to discuss. We don't need him buzzing around the door like a bee on a flower," she announced. "Now take a seat so we can get started." With that, she closed and locked the door behind them.

CHAPTER 44

Miss Mackie said, "Listen up. You need to know that this meeting is strictly confidential. Under no circumstances are you to share this information with anyone. Do not talk to your parents, other students, teachers, principals, or other family members. Don't even tell your pets or stuffed animals. Someone could be listening. Do I make myself clear? If you can't do that, then you need to leave now."

Spooky was still leaning against the back wall with her arms crossed and a scowl on her face. "What a bunch of bull crap," she exploded. "This is too funny. What could possibly be so important that we can't tell anyone?" She sort of snorted.

"Believe it or not, we are talking about Homeland Security and the safety of your families. In fact, we can only give you information on a need-to-know basis," shared Lisa.

Arthur nearly jumped to attention. His eyes had grown wide. His hands gripped the front edge of the desk in which he sat. "Homeland Security? This is the real thing, isn't it? I believe that, as a hall guard, I need to be in on this mission, whatever it is." He stood up, placed his hand over his heart, and stated, "I solemnly swear that I will abide by the rules you deem necessary for this mission."

"Oh, come on. Are you serious? This is like kiddy play," complained Spooky.

"I'm with Arthur on this one. I also swear to keep info to myself," stated Blossom as she stood.

Stinky and Carlos stood up at the same time. "Count us in," they declared.

"What is wrong with you? Can't you see they are making you look like fools?" fussed Spooky.

"I know something about acting foolish," Bull declared humbly. "If this will help me gain everyone's trust, then I'm in too. I also pledge my allegiance to the Homeland Security plan or whatever it is."

Spooky walked up to Pepper. "Pepper, it looks like you and I are the only sane students in this room. Come on, girlfriend, let's get out of here."

"I'm sorry, Spooky, I'm going join the cause. Haven't you noticed something odd is going on around the school? First, it was Bull, then Mr. Zornet started acting more peculiar than usual. For some bizarre reason, I have had the feeling that I'm being watched. Out of the corner of my eye, I have seen dark shadows move about, but only here at school. Truthfully, it scares me. I declare myself to the cause as well."

Open-mouthed, Spooky stared at the students. "You're all crazy as bedbugs." She made her way to the door. Her hand was almost on the doorknob when Miss Mackie spoke.

"Spooky, you don't have to believe that there is a threat. All you have to do is not share with others what you hear. My question to you is, wouldn't it be nice to be a part of a group that can make a difference? So what say you?"

Spooky stood with her hand only a fraction of an inch from the doorknob. Her hand dropped, and she turned around. She found a desk just outside the semicircle and sat down.

Miss Mackie studied her for a second then asked, "Does this mean you agree to keep information to yourself?"

Spooky nodded.

CHAPTER 45

There was click, followed by static, as the PA system snapped on.

"Your attention, attention, please. Mr. Zornet here. Anyone knowing the whereabouts of Mr. Teeterman, please buzz the office."

"*Wot, wot, wot,*" the secretary's voice could be heard in the background.

"What? That can't be true. Mackie told me that he wanted to talk to me," said Mr. Zornet.

"*Wot, wot, wot,*" answered the secretary.

"That crazy old bat. Wait until I get my hands…" The PA system clicked off.

"Students, I believe we are going to have a visitor," stated Miss Mackie in a calm voice.

Running feet could be heard coming down the hallway.

"Remain seated. I will be right back," said Miss Mackie.

Rattle, rattle, rattle. The doorknob sounded as though it might be ripped off the door. *Bam. Bam.*

Miss Mackie swung the door open. Mr. Zornet stumbled into the room in the middle of another bang on the door.

"By all means, do come in," declared Miss. Mackie.

Mr. Z stopped and straightened his shirt. "Mackie, you old witch, I should rip that ugly wig off your head and beat the crap out of you with it."

"Mr. Zornet, do you think this is the appropriate time and place for this discussion?" inquired Miss Mackie.

He stopped and looked at the students.

"This is not over, do you understand me, you daft old hag? I will get you for this." His voice started as a whisper but built in volume with his rage. "I will get you when you least expect it."

In a calm, quiet voice, she responded, "Thanks for giving me the heads up. I will keep a watch out for you."

"You're nuts, a complete lunatic, no, you're as cracked as a broken wingnut." He stormed away.

CHAPTER 46

As Miss Mackie pulled the door closed, she addressed the group of students. "It would seem that our first chore will be to find some way to keep Mr. Zornet busy during our mission. Does anyone have any ideas? Lisa, you make a list of the ideas."

"What if his car should happen to disappear?" asked App.

"Interesting idea. How might that happen?"

"I am a good driver. I could drive his car down to the church and hide it behind the dumpster."

"Good one," agreed Carlos. "I can slip his car keys out of his pocket. But I would need a distraction."

Bull piped up. "My parents are really angry about the grade I got in Zornet's class. He was the only teacher that wouldn't let me make up the work I missed. I can ask them to come up and talk to him. Do you think that will work?"

"That should work nicely," Carlos said with a smile.

"As a hall monitor, I can be in the halls after the bell rings. What if I delivered a note to Mr. Zornet, letting him know his car is missing?" added Arthur.

"Mr. Zornet fills his coffee cup every morning just before class. He spends the rest of the class sipping coffee. What if I hide his cup so he can't find it?" suggested Stinky.

The idea was added to the list.

Miss Mackie looked at Pepper. "Your job is going to be to convince Mr. Teeterman that we need to have all kinds of animals in the school."

"What? Why would I want to do that?"

"All I can tell you is that we need them here," answered Lisa.

"I suppose I could tell them I am doing a research project and need to observe student reaction to animals,"

"That sounds as if it might work," smiled Miss Mackie.

"I could pester him with a million questions every time I see him in the halls," offered Blossom.

"That should be effective," said Lisa, adding it to the growing list.

Spooky got up and joined the circle.

"It seems that I need to contribute to this effort. I'm a shadow. When he turns around, I'll be watching him. It is very effective at making people nervous. However, I will need to have freedom in the halls," she said as she looked at Arthur.

"You got it, sister."

The shadow idea was added to the list too.

"Students, I do believe we have a plan," declared Miss Mackie.

"Miss Mackie, may I share a few cautions?" asked Lisa.

"By all means."

"As time zero approaches, expect the unexpected. But don't let it frighten you. If you feel fear, hug an animal and show it love. Love is our ultimate defense. Most importantly, if you see a mist or specter, never ever let it know it has been seen," instructed Lisa. "Our code word from here on out will be storm or stormy. Like, it looks stormy, or there are lots of storms around the school."

"Any questions? Good, we're ready then," said Miss Mackie.

CHAPTER 47

*7:30 AM, three and one-half hours
until the time lines collide*

Lisa strolled into the kitchen. "Is everyone ready?"

"Yes, love. G and I will be at school to help with the arrival of the animals. The Humane Society, animal control, the nature center in Burton, Mott Farm and a local pet rescue will arrive at school between 10:00 and 10:15," declared Miss Pinky. "G and I will be at school at 9:30 to help get everyone settled in."

"See you then." Lisa and App left for school

7:40 AM

Mr. Zornet wandered the halls of Lamb School. He stopped to get a drink at the drinking fountain. He turned, water was still dripping off his chin, and he walked into Miss Mackie.

"Good morning, are you all ready for today?" she asked as she stared him in the eyes only a few inches from his nose.

"Yes, of course. Why do you ask?"

He backed up a step or two and bumped into the drinking fountain.

"Just wondering if you are ready. That's all."

Miss Mackie walked away. Mr. Zornet watched her go. He wiped the water from his mouth and shook his head. "Ready? Ready for what?" he asked.

Miss Mackie never answered.

He went to the office.

"Morning, Mr. Teeterman," uttered Mr. Z as he reached into his mailbox.

Someone was standing directly behind him. He turned and came face to face with Miss Mackie.

"Fine day, isn't it?" she stated.

"Yes, yes, just fine," Mr. Zornet confirmed as he moved out of her way.

He shook his head, grabbed his room key off the board, and hustled to his room. Once the door was unlocked, he clicked on the lights, took a deep breath, and let it out slowly. Mr. Z put his coat in the closet and went to his desk to pick up his coffee cup. It was nowhere to been seen.

"Where the heck is my coffee cup? I always put it right here."

"You seem a bit nervous this morning. Are you sure you are okay?" inquired Miss Mackie.

He spun around to find Miss Mackie standing behind him.

"What is wrong with you?"

"Me? Oh, I'm quite well. Thank you for asking."

He pointed to his desk and demanded in a harsh voice, "Did you take my coffee cup? It is always on my desk."

With a concerned look on her face, Miss Mackie looked at him and inquired, "Why would I know where you put your coffee cup?"

Mr. Z bared his teeth, drew a breath in between them, and growled. "I don't know why you are messing with me, but when I do find out, you are going to be sorry."

She patted him on the arm, "Really, my dear, you must calm down."

The PA system buzzed. The secretary's voice filled the room. "Mr. Zornet, you have parents that need to speak with you. Shall I send them up?"

"Yes, that would be fine."

"You will have to excuse me," he said to Miss Mackie. His eyes squinted in anger, "I have parents I need to speak to."

"I understand. I hope it goes well." She strolled out the door.

In the hall, she saw two parents with scowls on their faces, walking toward her. "Oh, you must be Bull's parents, Mr. and Mrs. Puckie. Mr. Zornet is right in this room." Miss Mackie departed as the nervous-sounding Mr. Zornet greeted them.

Miss Mackie stood at the end of the hallway and listened as Bull's folks yelled and bellowed at Mr. Zornet.

Coach walked up to Miss Mackie. "What is all that commotion in room 220?"

"Oh, nothing, really. Bull's parents are upset because Zornet won't let Bull make up the work he missed while he was sick."

"As department head, I will take care of this," he stated as he marched to Z's door and walked in.

"What seems to be the problem?"

All that could be heard of Bull's parents' comment was, "*Wot wot wot.*"

"Is that right? I understand completely. Mr. Zornet, these parents are correct. According to the school code of conduct, a student may make up work if he is sick. Bull was sick. End of discussion. Come, Mr. and Mrs. Puckie. I will walk you out."

Moments later, Mr. Z staggered out into the hall.

"You're looking a little pale," observed Miss Mackie. "Are you having a bad morning?"

He pushed past her with a coffee cup in his hand, "I found it, you crazy old bat. Did you think I wouldn't look in the file drawer?"

CHAPTER 48

8:00 AM, three hours left

The bell rang, and the students hurried into the building. Lisa and App passed Miss Mackie by her door. They tapped the side of their noses, and she gave a slight nod of her head in acknowledgement. The plan was in action.

Mr. Zornet filled his coffee cup and was hurrying to his post on the steps. He was late arriving because of the meeting with the Puckies. The students had filled the halls. He worked his way through the crowd, pushing between two girls deep in conversation, and he didn't stop to excuse himself but, instead, said, "Quit gossiping and get to class."

He tripped over a boy bending over to pick up a dropped book. "You fool. You nearly caused me to fall. Get out of the way." As Zornet walked away he mumbled to himself, "What a rotten way to start a day!"

He arrived at the arched window. "Pft. Now I'm too late to watch for those two miserable wretches."

He progressed on to his classroom doorway. Blossom stood at the door, waiting for him. "Mr. Zornet, I was wondering, how much coffee do you drink in one day?"

He looked confused. "What?"

"How much coffee do you drink in one day? I see you with a coffee cup in your hand all the time. Too much coffee is not good for you. It makes people jumpy. Did you know that?"

"What difference does it make to you?"

"I was concerned for your health. As you get older, you need to take better care of yourself. That is what we learned in health class. And I thought—"

"Blossom, go to class."

"But I—"

"Go. To. Class."

She scurried away.

Bull cleared the top of the steps, and he made his way toward Zornet, while Blossom kept him distracted. When Zornet turned to go into his room, there stood Bull.

"I'm here for my makeup work. Dad told me to pick it up."

Zornet took a deep breath and let it out slowly. "Not now. I haven't had a—"

Whop.

Carlos bumped into Zornet with the force of a runaway grocery cart. Z whirled around with the anger of a Tasmanian devil.

"What the heck is wrong with you? Why is everyone crazy today?"

Carlos backed away. Both hands up in the air. "My bad. I won't do it again."

"You better not, Carlos, or I will have you suspended." Zornet stalked into his classroom and slammed the door.

Carlos met App on the back steps. He passed Zornet's car keys to him and hurried into class. App headed to the parking lot. Arthur witnessed the exchange. He nodded his head at them and strolled away.

CHAPTER 49

9:30 AM, only ninety minutes before the timelines collide

Arthur trotted down the hallway. His smile nearly spread from ear to ear. At the intersection of the north-south and east-west hallways, he saw his team of misfits. He came to a sliding stop next to them. "I love it when a plan comes together," he quoted. He beamed at the crowd. "I always wanted to say that."

His statement was met with blank stares.

"Aww, come on. You recognize that statement, don't you?"

The group shook their heads no.

"Man, it is from the A-Team. You've seen the reruns, haven't you?"

Again, no response.

"You remember Mr. T and crazy Murdock, right?"

"Arthur, we need to get organized," scolded Pepper.

"Gee whiz, the only time I'm able to use a great quote, and no one but me appreciates it. It kind of loses some of the fun," he mumbled.

Pepper checked her clipboard of assignments.

"Mr. G and Miss Pinky, you will assist the animals coming through the front door. All of those animals will go upstairs." She handed them a list of teachers and classrooms.

App came hustling toward the group. "The item was placed down at the church as planned," he said as he passed the keys back to Carlos.

"Good work, App," said Pepper. "You are back just in time to help unload animals. You and Lisa will be stationed at the south doors. Your rooms for delivery are downstairs."

She handed them their list of rooms and teachers.

"Stormy and Bull, I want you to take the north door. Your rooms will be the north-south hall on the main floor, and Arthur and Carlos will deliver the animals on the east-west hall. Arthur will have to cover for Carlos while he returns the keys. Will that be a problem?"

Arthur answered Pepper with a salute. "No problem."

"Okay. I believe we are as ready as we can be. If you have any questions or need help, I will be here on the main floor. Good luck, everyone," Pepper stated with a nervous note to her voice.

CHAPTER 50

The nature center had several cages with assorted animals, but the one that captured Lisa and App's attention was a rather large, covered bird cage.

App tried to peek into the cage. "Wow, what kind of bird is that?"

"It's a raven," replied the naturalist.

"That's unusual. How did you acquire a raven?" Lisa asked. "Did you raise it from a baby?"

"That is a funny story. About six weeks ago, a group of us at the center went out to the picnic table to eat lunch. After eating, one of the maintenance guys asked if anyone wanted to play black jack.

"This raven lands on the table and looked at him. It walks over to the dealer and pulled cards out of his hand. The big bird turned and looked at me with its beady eyes, ruffled its long neck feathers, then walked over to where I sat. It was very eerie, the way it looked at me.

The man from the nature center shifted his weight from one foot to the other. He pulled at his collar as he relived the incident. "I had a stick of beef jerky in my hand, and the raven walked over to me and said, 'Want some. Want some.' He looked me in the eyes. It was as though I had known the bird all my life. I handed him a piece of the jerky. He has been with me ever since."

Lisa and App shared a stunned look at each other.

"Wow, that is quite a story," stated Lisa. "May we see him?"

"Sure. No problem," said the naturalist as he removed the cover from the cage.

A very inquisitive raven looked back at them.

App watched the bird for a moment then asked, "What is its name?"

"We call him Black-Jack. It was so odd for him to land on the table at the exact time as the maintenance man said black jack, don't you think?

"*Trp, trp, trp,*" said the bird. The bird fluffed its long neck feathers and stared at them with his beady black eyes. He shook his head and said, "I love you."

Lisa smiled at the bird and quietly said, "I love you too."

CHAPTER 51

It was the final trip out to the cars and vans that brought the animals to Lamb School. A guinea pig snuggled under G-Master's chin as he walked back in the front doors of the school.

"Aren't you just the cutest little thing?" G told the pig.

"*Pt, pt, pt, pt,*" answered the guinea pig as he soaked up the attention that G gave him.

"Ya know, your hair is the same color as mine. Even better, it sticks up like mine too. Say, maybe we are related," laughed G at his own joke.

The pig took a hold of G's collar and started to chew.

"Hey, little buddy. That's about enough of that," he softly scolded the rodent. One-handed, he tucked his collar in so the little critter couldn't gnaw a hole in it. "I guess you don't like my jokes, eh?"

G pulled the school door open and stepped inside. He witnessed the evil mist at work. He immediately moved out of sight to assess the situation. "Did you just see what I saw? It looks like you arrived not a moment too soon," he whispered to his little buddy.

Pepper backed herself into the corner created by the door and the wall next to the second set of fire doors. She held a clipboard crushed to her chest and stared at the wall across the hall. In front of her was a wisp of the evil mist. She looked away. It danced about like the smoke of a fire. Once in a while, it would sway her direction. She stood still as a statue but made no eye contact.

G-Master held the guinea pig securely in his arm, stepped out from behind the front door, and walked up to Pepper.

"Hi there. I'm App and Lisa's father." He extended his hand, but she didn't move. "Say, aren't you the girl that set up this research project?"

She nodded her head.

Vapors continued to sway and spin between them.

"Ya know, sometimes putting together a project like this can create a stormy mess."

At the word stormy, Pepper's eyes grew large. "Yes! Yes it can. Does it look stormy to you too?" she asked in one big rush of air.

"Aye, lass, it does. I have a little friend here that needs to be taken to room 202. Don't forget to hold him close and give him lots of love." He handed the rodent to Pepper.

The word "love" made the devilish mist jerk back a bit.

"Oh, isn't he just a little sweet pea?" gushed Pepper as she lovingly rubbed her cheek against his soft fur.

Poof! The mist disappeared.

Pepper relaxed just a tad. "It isn't stormy anymore, is it?"

G-Master smiled at her and said, "Nope, it is all clear. Job well done. Keep your little buddy with you until this project is over."

"Thank you so much," Pepper said as she headed up the stairs.

Miss Mackie had heard their conversation and stepped out into the hall. "Hmmm, maybe this plan will work," she said as she closed her classroom door behind her.

CHAPTER 52

Twenty minutes to zero hour, outside of the school

*R*ing. Ring. Ring.

"Nine-one-one, what is your emergency?"

"Lamb School is missing!"

"Pardon me. Did you say Lamb School is missing?"

"Yes, ma'am."

"The Lamb School on Barnes in Burton?"

"Yes, ma'am."

"How do you know it is missing?"

"I'm sitting in my car, across the street from where it should be, and it's not there."

"Have you been drinking or taken any medication that might cause you to not see things clearly?"

"No, ma'am."

"Hang on, I will get a police car dispatched to your location. Dispatch. This is nine–one-one, we need a cruiser sent to Lamb School. We have a report that the school is missing."

"*What?*"

"You heard me. I have a lady on the line that believes the school is missing. She may need some medical assistance."

"It's kind of early in the day for this kind of foolishness. It must be a full moon. I'll check it out."

"Thanks, I'll keep her on the phone until you can get there."

"Hello, ma'am, are you okay?"

"Yes, I'm just worried about all the students in the building."

"When did the school go missing?"

"I'm not really sure. You see, I am the crossing guard. The school was there at eight o'clock this morning. I helped the little kids cross the road."

"Excuse me, *you're* the crossing guard?"

"Yes, ma'am. I know the school was there until at least nine. I left and went to get a doughnut and coffee. I came back to the school. I'm a homeroom mother in my grandson's class. I'm supposed to help with the animals in his class today. But the school is gone."

"What can you see?"

"A very thick fog."

"Did you try the door?"

"No, ma'am, I couldn't."

"Why couldn't you try the door?"

"This may sound a bit odd, but the fog wouldn't let me through. Oh, I hear the police siren. They're here now. I have to go."

Click!

CHAPTER 53

Twenty minutes to zero hour, inside of the school

*C*rackle, buzzzz, sizzle—

"This dang PA system"—*crackle, zzzzzz*—"can't get it to—"

"*Wot, wot, wot, wot,*" the secretary could be heard talking in the background.

"What did you say? It's working? What's working?" said Teeterman.

"*Wot, wot.*"

"The PA is working? Is that what you said? Oh, oh, oh," he stammered.

"Your attention, attention please. This is Mr. Teeterman."

Spooky rolled her eyes and said, "Like duh, who else would it be?" She was standing in the hall with Bull at the north door. They had made their last trip out to the truck to bring the last of the animals into the school.

"I have never met anyone that loves to hear himself talk as much as he does. Doesn't he just drive you crazy with all his announcements?"

"What announcements?" inquired Bull.

"Oh, for goodness' sake, will you stop playing with that rat and pay attention," fussed Spooky.

Zzzz, pop, pop—"We are experiencing difficulty with the electrical systems in the—"

The lights flashed on and off twice then stayed on.

"—it is important that everyone remains calm. Be sure the animals are kept quiet. Just a minute."

"*Wot, wot, wot,*" said the secretary.

"Well, by all means. I was just handed an animal protocol sheet to read. '*For the safety of the animals and fellow students during this program, please follow these procedures: stay calm, hold the animal close, and be sure to give it reassurance so it feels protected. Remember, always stay calm.*'"

CHAPTER 54

Fifteen minutes

Blossom made her way to Zornet's door. She knocked and waited for a reply.

Making his way to the door, Mr. Zornet muttered to himself, "Animals all over the school. This is the most asinine thing I have ever seen. Mr. Teeterman must be an idiot to allow this."

Zornet grabbed the doorknob and pushed the door open violently.

"What the heck do you want now?" he angrily demanded. "I have had it with all these foolish questions and interruptions."

"Why, Mr. Zornet, are you having a bad day? I'm sorry, but I'm afraid that this note isn't going to help."

"Give me that," he said as he snatched it out of her hand.

Blossom took a step back as he opened the note and began to read.

> To: Zornet
> From: Teeterman
> It was reported that your car is missing from the teacher's parking lot. You might want to check this out at your earliest convenience.

Lester Zornet cut loose with monstrous rage. "If I get my hands on the one that took my car, I will kill them!"

His eyes took on an unnatural look. Where the eyes should be white, his were red. The iris of his eyes had all but disappeared. They were black, with an empty, unfocused look. He was shaking from head to toe.

Zornet's frenzied behavior drew all the evil darkness to the second floor, like fresh dog poop draws flies. The hallway developed a smell of rotten eggs. Or maybe it was more the smell of a musty, moldy, damp basement. Whatever it was, it made Blossom want to gag as she backed away toward the stairs. The air was heavy and dense. It felt oppressive, and it was difficult to breathe.

Zornet's wrath continued. The blue veins in his neck stood out, like overfilled water balloons. His contorted face moved about, as the muscles under the skin bunched and tightened.

The lights blinked off for a second. When they turned back on, the mist boiled around him. It rolled and cracked like a whip at the edges. Images of trapped souls bent in close to Zornet. They hissed and chattered at him. Greedy hands reached out to touch him.

"I'm somebody! I'm not invisible! I will be treated with respect!" screamed Mr. Z.

"Let me in," hissed the mist, "and I can give you the power to be all you want to be." It shimmered and twirled faster and faster around him.

"That is exactly what I want. Yes, I want the power. I will show them all!" he ranted.

Blossom walked backward, all the way to the stairs. She turned then and ran down, taking two or three steps at a time.

"Miss Mackie! Miss Mackie!" she yelled. "Come quick. It didn't work! It didn't work."

Miss Mackie came out of her room, like the devil was on her tail. She met Blossom at the bottom of the stairs. "What happened?"

"He didn't leave the building like we planned. He went crazy instead. He was pulling the drinking fountain off the wall by the time I got to the stairs."

Crash—bang—echoed down the stairwell.

116

"Oh, dear," stated Miss Mackie. "Go get Lisa and App. I will see what I can do."

Blossom hesitated a second.

"Go!" yelled Mackie, as she seemed to fly up the steps.

CHAPTER 55

Ten minutes

Black-Jack was a great success in the art room. Once he was out of the cage, he flew around the room. He landed on the teacher's head and stole her glasses. After dropping them on the floor, he landed on the teacher's desk and ripped the pages out of her plan book.

The class went wild with laughter. Even Lisa and App hung around to see what the silly raven would do next.

Black-Jack swooped down, snatched a bead out of one girl's hair, and dropped it down the sink drain. *Kur-plunk.*

Lisa and App laughed at Black-Jack's hilarious antics.

In the middle of the laughter, Lisa felt a shimmer of menacing apprehension. The hair on her arms stood up, and her skin shivered with goose bumps. Sinister evil was active. She grabbed App by the arm as she ran past him.

"Something is very wrong," was all she said as she made for the door.

Black-Jack sat on the shoulder of the naturalist as he explained how he met the bird. Black-Jack's attention was on Lisa. When she and App rushed to the door, the raven took to the air. It circled the room once. When the door opened, the bird followed them out.

Up the stairs, to the main floor, Lisa tracked the feeling of anger and disturbance. Lisa and App met up with Blossom in front of the office.

"Get the team and meet us on the second floor as soon as you can!" yelled Lisa to Blossom as they ran past her. She and App continued up the stairs.

CHAPTER 56

Three minutes

Water shot out from the pipes in the wall, where the drinking fountain had been attached. It shot across the hall and hit the lockers. The flooded corridor became a river. Water splashed over the steps like a waterfall.

Miss Mackie waded through the rush of water to the second floor. One step from the top, she froze. "Oh, my goodness," she said. She took a deep breath and stepped on the top step.

"Lester Zornet, you must stop before it is too late," Miss Mackie called up to him.

Mr. Zornet levitated about three feet off the floor. He was tightly wrapped in black mist that swirled around him. Flashes of electricity snapped and crackled in the evil blackness. He held up his hand, and it crackled from his fingertips.

Bodaks were on the walls and ceiling, crawling with long, spidery, boney fingers. Their skeleton faces had empty eye sockets, and yet they held a strange, red-glow. Their mouths chattered open and closed with excitement of the upcoming doom. They oozed out from behind the lockers. Bony hands reached up and out between the cracks in the floor tiles. With hands placed flat on the floor, they pulled their bodies out.

"I see it now. I have always been the great one. Everyone has tried to hide it." He looked in Miss Mackie's direction.

"*You, you* ugly *old* hag are the worst. You have looked down your twisted scarred nose at me ever since I was hired. *Not* anymore."

"Lester, that is enough. Come down here at once."

"How dare you speak to me in such a manner! I am your superior, and don't you ever forget it."

Lisa and App rounded the corner in time to hear the exchange between him and Mackie.

"He is delusional," whispered App to Lisa.

Crouching low to stay out of his line of sight, they slowly eased their way closer. Black-Jack landed on Lisa's shoulder and cuddled up next to her. Classroom doors opened, as teachers investigated the cause of all the disruption.

"Stay in your rooms," commanded Zornet with an angry bark. Classroom doors slammed shut. "Ha ha ha! Finally, everyone understands I have the power."

He looked back at Miss Mackie, "You will bow down and call me Master."

"I won't ever do that," stated Mackie in a calm voice.

He shot a bolt of electricity at her. She stepped to the side. It missed and hit the wall. Pieces of brick broke free and flew through the air.

Lisa was now directly behind Zornet. She reached up to grab his foot but stopped when Miss Mackie shook her head no. Lisa faltered a moment and returned to her position by the wall.

Zornet saw Mackie shake her head. He spun himself a quarter turn so he could see them both.

"Ahh, Miss Lisa Time. So good of you to join us. I have been waiting for you. Now I understand how you could be in two places at once. You think you are so smart. It shall be my pleasure to take care of you as well."

Miss M moved quick for someone so old. She made a lunge toward the angry teacher and slipped in the water. She fell to the floor. Before she could regain her footing, he turned and snapped a bolt of electricity at her.

Zow, snap!

The water on the floor made the zap of electricity lethal. Miss Mackie was instantly killed.

"No!" screamed Lisa as she ran to Miss Mackie's side.

She felt for a pulse. There was none. As if in slow motion, Lisa stood. She turned toward the dark enemy. Black-Jack remained tightly perched on her shoulder. She made direct eye contact with Zornet and never blinked. Her hands were in fists at her sides, and her lips were pressed into a straight line.

"Haw, haw," he laughed. "Well, little girl, I wonder what you think you can do to me? I have great power."

She took a step toward him. Again, he laughed at her.

"We have been waiting a long time for this little dance, haven't we? I told you long ago I'd be back for you," came a strange voice from Mr. Zornet's that wasn't his.

She said not a word but took another step closer.

App and the misfits stood helplessly, watching the exchange between Lisa and App. App yelled, "Lisa, don't!"

Lisa was so lost in her anger and focused on Zornet, she didn't hear him.

Zornet taunted her with an evil sneer, "Little missy thinks she is all grown up and can take on all the power of evil and darkness all by her little self."

The evil mist around him was in a frenzy. It hissed and popped.

"Oh, let's just stop this foolishness." He raised his right hand above his head and brought it down with a snap. The power was so great, he needed his left hand to hold his right hand straight.

Lisa braced herself for the hit. She raised her hands up and deflected the blast. The bolt ricocheted off her hands without causing her any injuries. It flashed back at Zornet and hit him in the chest before he knew what happened.

At the exact instant of impact, the three time glitches collided. The flash of blue-white lights screamed through the building, blinding the witnesses. There was a resounding explosion that shook the school to its foundation. Mr. Zornet disintegrated into a pulpy gray ash. For a fraction of a moment, his outline hung in the air.

Then along with the evil mist, the bodaks, and his ashes were sucked into another time period.

Lisa collapsed to the floor beside Miss Mackie and cried. The team of misfits gathered around her to give emotional support. Black-Jack disappeared.

EPILOGUE

The day was sunny but cool, with an occasional puffy cloud in the sky. The hearse was followed by several cars as it wound its way through the cemetery. It stopped on the hill, close to the open grave site. Mourners exited their cars and waited for Miss Mackie's casket to be removed from the back of the hearse.

Bull, Arthur, and Carlos were pallbearers, along with Mr. Teeterman, Mr. Hub, and Coach. When the back door opened, they stepped into position, took ahold of the brass handles, and carried Miss Mackie to her final resting place.

Lisa followed along with the other mourners. Tears streamed down her face.

I'm such a failure, she thought. She hung her head and sobbed.

App stepped up beside her and put an arm around her. She turned toward him and placed her head on his chest. They both wept and held each other for comfort.

G took a step toward her, and Pinky stopped him with a touch of her hand.

"I need to go and take care of my girl," he said, with a tear shimmering in his eye.

"Yes, I know, love, but I think App is who she needs right now," Pinky said.

"Oh," replied G.

Once the casket was placed on the stand over the open grave, the preacher began to speak, "Dear friends, we gather together here today to say goodbye to Miss Ismay Mackie. She dedicated her life—"

"Lisa, Lisa, look at me."

"Black-Jack?"

"Yes, dear."

"But I recognize your voice. You're—You have the voice of the Wise One."

"Yes, dear."

Lisa looked around at the others standing near her.

"Don't worry about them, love. I look as though I am standing in the crowd, but I'm really in your mind."

There was a flurry of rainbow sprinkles, and Black-Jack changed into a lovely lady. She had mocha-colored skin and kind, loving eyes. Long, black hair fell past her shoulders, and she wore a shimmering blue-black gown, just like Black-Jack's feathers.

"You are very distressed, so I thought it might be better for you to see me in human form."

"You're Black-Jack?"

"Yes, love."

"So you were with us the entire time?"

"Yes, dear. Remember I told you I understand time travel and time glitches, but I didn't understand people. That is why I needed you."

"Oh."

"Why are you in such torment? You did a perfect job. You made wise choices and handled difficult situations."

"How can you say that?" cried Lisa, with yet another flood of tears in her eyes. Because of me, two people died. I didn't do anything right."

"Oh no, child. You have that all wrong. What you did was save hundreds of people. If you had failed, the school and all those in it would have perished. In fact, most of Burton and the surrounding area would have been gone."

"But Miss Mackie and Mr. Zornet?"

"You couldn't have saved Mr. Zornet. He made bad choices long ago, and for that, he had to pay. Miss Mackie had been around for countless years, but you know that. She was ready for a rest. In fact, when she met you, she put a request in for retirement. She felt you would be able to accomplish much. She said that you are the future. You are much more than you seem."

"But?"

"No buts. This was her idea."

"You mean she didn't have to go?"

"Indeed, she did not. She did, however, want you to have this."

Black-Jack placed a brilliant crystal in Lisa's hand. "This is very special. It is the symbol of the Old Order of the Wise Ones. When a Wise One retires, they are encouraged to pass it on to someone deserving. She picked you. That is a true honor. There hasn't been anyone deserving in several hundred years."

"I don't know what to say."

"Then say nothing. The service is almost over. You need to return to the moment." With that, Black-Jack changed back into a raven and flew away.

"Would anyone like to share?" asked the preacher.

Everyone stood still.

"I would," said Lisa as she dried her eyes. "Miss Mackie didn't have any family. What she did have was a small band of students that she helped bring together as a team." Lisa nodded at App, Arthur, Pepper, Spooky, Carlos, Blossom, Bull, and Stinky. "Our lives are better for having known her."

In the distance, a raven called out a farewell.

Bodak ('boʊdæk/ BO-dak) are undead, fantasy creatures from the infinite layers of the abyss. They are drawn to areas of impending destruction. If eye contact is made, they will suck your soul out of you while you are still alive.

ABOUT THE AUTHOR

L ois is a proud resident of Michigan and uses her state as the setting for her books. She is a retired teacher and enjoys writing fantasy books for children and young-at-heart adults. She lives in Lennon, Michigan, with her husband and a menagerie of pets.

Also, by Lois Farley-Ray

****

A Glitch in Time

CPSIA information can be obtained
at www.ICGtesting.com
Printed in the USA
FSHW010218110220
66993FS

9 781646 285693